Abraham de Sola

Biography of David Aaron de Sola

Late Senior Minister of the Portuguese Jewish Community in London

Abraham de Sola

Biography of David Aaron de Sola
Late Senior Minister of the Portuguese Jewish Community in London

ISBN/EAN: 9783337071301

Printed in Europe, USA, Canada, Australia, Japan

Cover: Foto ©Raphael Reischuk / pixelio.de

More available books at **www.hansebooks.com**

BIOGRAPHY

OF

DAVID AARON DE SOLA,

LATE SENIOR MINISTER OF THE PORTUGUESE JEWISH
COMMUNITY IN LONDON.

BY HIS SON,

THE REV. DR. ABRAHAM DE SOLA,

OF MONTREAL.

.

PHILADELPHIA:
WM. H. JONES & SON, PRINTERS,
No. 510 MINOR STREET.
5624.

DEDICATION.

To the cherished memory of a beloved father, revered teacher, and pious exemplar;—to a dear mother, his much-prized and loved helpmeet, as a memento of her deep solicitude and devotion;—to his uniformly warm and zealous friend, SIR MOSES MONTEFIORE, Israel's champion, who, with his lamented consort, THE LADY JUDITH, ה"ע, were, from first to last, the main supporters and encouragers of his literary and all other undertakings;—in grateful recognition of this and numerous other tokens of more than a friend's kindness to himself and family, I dedicate the present faint sketch of one whose name will ever be associated with the respect which wisdom, virtue, and piety command from their admirers.

ABRAHAM DE SOLA.

MONTREAL, Kislev, 5625.

BIOGRAPHY

OF

DAVID AARON DE SOLA,

LATE SENIOR MINISTER OF THE PORTUGUESE JEWISH COMMUNITY
IN LONDON.

———— —— ————

BY HIS SON, THE REV. DR. ABRAHAM DE SOLA, OF MONTREAL.

———— ——— ————

DAVID AARON DE SOLA was descended from an ancient family of Sephardim, who emigrated from Spain in 1492, on the expulsion of the Jews from that country, by Ferdinand and Isabella. The family seem to have settled mainly in Holland; but their name appears at a very early period of the re-establishment of the Jewish community in England, under Charles II. It may be permitted us, as preliminary to the biographical sketch we attempt, to give a brief account of some of the members of this family which, both in Holland and England, has produced for us so many ministers and scholars of repute. We shall only refer to such members of the Holland branch as were connected with the early history and training of the subject of this notice.

In the first row of graves in what used to be called the New Burial Ground at Mile End, London, is the tombstone of Isaac de Sola, who was preacher in London in 5450–5460 (1690–1700), consequently, only some thirty-five years after the re-admission of Jews into England, under Charles II, and before any of the existing Synagogues had been built—the most ancient, that of the Portuguese in Bevis Marks, having been erected in 1701. He died Hesvan 5495 (1735), as is recorded on his tombstone. He

was the author of the following works in Spanish : 1, A volume
of Sermons,* printed in Amsterdam 5464 (1704). 2, Elucidations
of mooted points of law,† Amsterdam, 5464. 3, Exposition of the
Psalms. 4, " Questions and Replies " on the Pentateuch. 5, Another volume of " Questions and Replies," for pulpit purposes.
6, A Collection of twenty-one Sermons preached in Amsterdam.
The first of these works, which displays deep theological research
and a wide acquaintance with general literature, contains the unqualified approval of the communal chief Rabbi and Principal of
the Rabbinical College, the celebrated Haham Selomoh de Oliveyra,‡ as also the warm eulogium of " the honored Haham and
learned preacher," R. Selomoh Yehuda Leon Templo, author of
the well-known " Reshith Chochmah ;"§ the latter styles our author his " esteemed and intelligent disciple," and speaks of his
earliest productions|| in the most laudatory terms.¶ He was about

---

* " Sermones hechos sobre diferentes asumptos." Compuestos y Predicados
por el Docto Ingenio Ishac De Sola, En Amsterdam año 5464. En casa de
Mosch Diaz. They were chiefly delivered in the *Yesiba Liryat Hen*, and *Yesiba Baalé Teshuba*, Amst., and are dedicated to Jacob. Abm. Nunes Hen-
riques.

† " Preguntas con sus Respuestos." Hechas en la *Yesiba de Livyat Hen*, en
las Festividades del año. Por el estudioso Ishac De Sola. Amst. 5464. M. Diaz.

‡ This learned Rabbi, whose reputation in the eminent Amsterdam school
stands second only to that of the historical Menasseh ben Israel, and who was
the attached friend of Isaac De Sola, was " a theologian, astronomer, moral-
philosopher, and grammarian of great repute." (Vide De Rossi, " Diz. Stor.
degli Autori Ebrei," vol. ii. p. 81, Parma ed. ; Lindo's " Jews of Spain," &c.,
p. 368, and Zinn's " Sephardim," p. 464.) He was author of the following
highly esteemed works in Hebrew and Portuguese : 1, יד לשון Hebrew Grammar. 2, דל שפתים Chaldee Grammar. 3, בית רענן Hebrew and Portuguese
Vocabulary. 4, אילן וענפיו Port. and Heb. Vocabulary. 5, עץ חיים Scripture
Roots. 6, אילת אהבים Hebrew Rhetoric. 7, שרשות נבלות Hebrew Poetry. 8,
דרכי ה' on the Precepts. 9, רבי נוים Rabbinical Logic, &c.

§ ראשית חכמה " Gramathica Hebrayca," &c. Amst. Athias 5463.

|| On page 37 of No. 1 he himself says : " Ofreciendo estas primicias q'en la
primavera de mis verdes estudios cogi del jardin de la divina ley, a la houra(?)
de los M. M. Ss. Parnassim y Gabay desta Santa *Yesiba*."

¶ Pois os primeyros lavores descobre tantos visos, como contem estes Sermoins, &c., tuó admiravis em tudo, na fulileza do engenho, na fineza do dis-
curso, no eloquente do estilo, no pezo das razoins, & pureza das palavras que
mais paresem discurços de hum pregador provecto, que Sermoins de hum *en-
tendimento principiante*, &c.

twenty-five years old when he published his first volume of Sermons, and appears then to have been married,* was in London in 1704,† went to Amsterdam the same year, and had also visited Bayonne, since one of his Sermons (No. 10) was delivered there before the "K. K. Nefutsoth Yehudah," whence we may conclude that he enjoyed an extensive reputation as preacher. A period of thirty-one years intervened between the publication of this volume and his decease, which was in Hesvan, 5495, when he had not yet attained his sixtieth year. His reputation was shared by his, we believe, only son, Abraham De Sola, (Hazan and Beth Din of the London Portuguese community,) who as Hebrew scholar and theologian had but few superiors in his day. The name of his wife Abigail appears in the list of those who bequeathed legacies to the Congregational Orphan Society,‡ of which charity she was a warm friend. They are interred in the same Beth Haim, and near their graves is that of another friend to the communal institutions, Elias De Sola, who died 5571 (1811); but as the subject of this notice had, at this period, already attained his thirteenth year, we will now revert to such members of his family in Holland as were connected with his early history.

Dr. Benjamin De Sola, Court Physician to William V., Prince of Orange, and Stadthouder of the Netherlands, was an eminent practitioner at the Hague, and received his secular training at the University of Utrecht—enlightened Holland imposing no religious tests or civil disqualifications on her Jewish population, to prevent their attaining the highest pinnacle of political and intellectual distinction. A striking and interesting proof of this is afforded in the Inaugural Medical Dissertation which he wrote in Latin§ previous to his obtaining his degree of M. D., a copy of which lies before us, printed in 1773. The title-page shows that

---

* Page 56.
† "En el poco tiempo que assisti en aquella ponpulosa ciudad de Londres."
‡ See Report of the Society, issued in 1825.
§ "Dissertatio Medica Inauguralis de Matris præ Alieno Nutricis Lactis Necessitate ac Utilitate, quam annuente Summo Numine * * * nec non amplissimi Senatus Academici consensu, atque Nobilissimæ Facultatis Medicæ decreto, pro gradu Doctoratus. Eruditorum Examini submittit *Benjamin de Sola*, Amstelodamensis, Die xxix. Decembris MDCCLXXIII. H. L. Q. S." It is accompanied with a copperplate vignette of Utrecht University, &c.

he was "candidate for the highest honors and privileges in Medicine,"* which he in fact obtained; and although he wrote this treatise "*ex auctoritate Rectoris Magnifici Joannis Henrici Voorda J. U. P. et Juris Civilis Professoris Ordinarii,*" still he does not dedicate it to that high functionary, but to three of his co-religionists. He exhibits his respectful consideration for the religious chief of his Synagogue by dedicating it first to the Haham, S. Salem ("*viro venerabili cruditissimo,*" &c.), next to his chief instructor, Jacob de Meza, a Jewish physician (*Med. Doctori expertissimo studiorum suorum ductori fidelessimo*), and lastly to his fellow-student, J. Belmonte (*Alumno suo dilectissimo*). A noteworthy fact, proving his Hebrew attainments and his independence in treating his subject, not less than the enlightened liberality which obtained in his Alma Mater and among the literati around him, is that he supports his line of argument not merely by reference to Latin and Greek authors, but also by the Hebrew commentators.† This learned and eminent man, to whose high reputation the literature of the day bears ample testimony, became so much attached to, and favorably impressed with his nephew David, that he took him at the early age of eleven years to train him for his profession; but after studying osteology for some time, our young student preferred to devote himself exclusively to his favorite theology and Hebrew literature. In 1814, Dr. Benjamin De Sola having had the misfortune to become blind, went to Amsterdam, and underwent there an operation which partially restored his sight. A brother having died at Curaçoa who left him a considerable legacy, he went to reside there; but did not survive his arrival above a year. His remaining brother in Amsterdam, David Aaron De Sola,‡ who was distinguished for his Jewish learning, had four sons,§ the eldest of whom, Aaron,‖

---

* "Summisque in Medecina Honoribus Privilegiis, rite ac legitime consequendis.

† See pp. 11, 12. At the end of the Treatise is a rythmic Eulogy by another friend and co-religionist, A. Coronel, M. D.

‡ Ob. 5558. He married Sarah Jessurun d'Oliveyra, Ob. 5568.

§ Aaron, Moses, Isaac, and Samuel.

‖ Born 1770, died 13th June, 1821.

married Sarah Namias Torres,* by whom he had issue two daugh-
ters† and one son, the subject of this sketch.

David Aaron de Sola.was born in Amsterdam on the 26th day
of Kislev, 5557 (26th Dec. 1796). His parents were highly edu-
cated persons, whose intelligence was only exceeded by their
piety and scrupulous observance of their religious duties. The
then Chief Rabbi of Amsterdam, Haham Daniel Cohen D'Azavedo, styles the father "a man of superior intelligence, perfect
and upright." ‡איש תם וישר הוא נכרא פרישא And of the mother,
whose Hebrew attainments were deemed extraordinary even in a
community where female proficiency in the sacred language was
by no means a rarity, he writes, "She was in truth 'a virtuous
woman,' who was constantly employed in the study of sacred
literature, until her soul went to heaven some years since."
וכנאכמת היהה אשת חיל דלא פסיק גרכא כפוכמא יום ולילה בכפרי קרש כידי יום*
ויום וכחרש לחדש עד אשר יעלתה נשכתה לשמים לקצות שנים §

On their only son these gifted parents lavished their best care,
so that at a very early age his progress in Hebrew and general
literature was very great. His mother's chief delight was to
watch and further this progress, and the development of pious
principles, by unceasing exertions; and he never forgot her unceasing solicitude, but to the latest day of his life always spoke
of her in the warmest terms of affection and reverence. The an-
nual mortuary service he held for her was always a melancholy
occasion for him. The memory of such a mother in Israel is indeed blessed.

Long before he attained his religious majority he was competent to act as *Baal Koreh.* His Hebrew grammatical studies
commenced with Templo's ראשית חכמה and were continued in the
more elaborate works of De Balmis, Lumbroso, M. Kimchi, and
Redak. These studies branched out to Hebrew Poetry, which he
read with great avidity, becoming well acquainted with that glo-
rious band of Spanish-Jewish poets whose productions have never
been excelled. The regular reading and translation of the sacred

---

* On 2d Tamuz, 5553.

† The first died prematurely, the second married Heer Jacob J. Bassan, an
eminent mathematician in Amsterdam.

‡ See his תהלה לדוד   § Ibid.

Scriptures, with their exposition, formed an essential part of his
early training. In the pious and happy home of Aaron and Sarah De Sola the favorite volume which invariably made its appearance on Sabbath evenings was the "*Paraphrasis Commenta-
rio*" of R. Isaac Aboab, an excellent work written in Spanish,
and a favorite expositor among the Sephardim of Amsterdam.
This book, diligently studied as it was, would in itself have afforded him considerable acquaintance with Jewish interpretation ;
but his father, who designed for him a thorough theological training, soon introduced him to the original Hebrew sources, and he
thus speedily became acquainted with the Commentaries of Kimchi, Aben Ezra, Rashi, Nachmanides, and the Midrashim. The
philosophical acumen and beautiful style of Abarbanel always
rendered him, even in later days, a favorite author. His father,
a great Talmudist, soon had the pleasure of seeing him devote
himself to the higher branches of Hebrew theology, and in the
Beth-Hamidrash he studied with great assiduity the Talmud,*
Turim, and later Possekim. He was admitted in the Medras at the
unusually early age of eleven years, and continued his attendance
there for nearly nine years. During this time he was promoted
through all the five degrees, up to the highest, which could only
be attained by *public* competition among the students (*escuchas*).†
Of this famous Jewish College he himself gives us a brief notice
when in 1854 he contributed to the Jewish papers an interesting
account of the visit of the king of Portugal and suite to the Amsterdam Portuguese Synagogue. He says :

"His Majesty next proceeded to the ancient and famous Beth
Hamedrash 'Ets Hayim,' which, with its valuable library, is in
one of the buildings forming the spacious quadrangle in which
the Synagogue stands. There are two Medrashim, several religious schools, and Yeshiboth. This seminary is famous for the
many celebrated and erudite theologians who have therein flourished. Of these it is only necessary to mention Menasseh ben Is-

---

* From a memorandum made by himself in a volume of the Talmud we find
that *Moed Katon* and *Betzah* were the treatises read by him in his earlier years,
while yet in the *Medras Pequeno* or Junior Seminary. Another volume of the
Talmud shows he had studied *Massecheth Megillah* in 5575, when in his seven-
teenth year.

† See Letter to the Velhos, 1st of March, 1854.

rael, Saul Levy Morteira, Raphael de Aguilar, Sasportas, Athias, Oliveyra, Meldola, &c. The volumes of doctrinal decisions published under the title of ע"ות פרי עץ חיים contain the works of the more-modern theologians who have there studied."

In this eminent seminary of Jewish learning he was constantly to be found. "His youth," writes Chief Rabbi D'Azavedo, "was passed within the walls of the College or of the Synagogue. In either of these was he always to be found from the time that his mind developed itself and he left his mother's care.*" It is not surprising that as the result of this close application, joined to great intellectual gifts, we should find so, competent and trustworthy authority as Haham D'Azavedo pronounce him a thorough Talmudist, a title which at that time and in that community was not bestowed on smatterers, but only on those who by years of successful study had rendered themselves worthy of distinction. He applies to him the flattering titles נבון וחכם פלפלא חריפא. He also speaks in laudatory terms of his general attainments, and presented him with a diploma such as few young men under the age of twenty had there received. He pronounces him to the fullest extent competent to discharge Rabbinical functions, to examine Shochetim in their duties, both theoretically and practically, and to assume the ministerial office "in every city and every place."

But while he was thus assiduously pursuing his theological studies, his secular training was not at all neglected. The Spanish and Portuguese languages being commonly spoken in his father's house, and being in fact the chief medium of religious instruction both in the Synagogue and Beth Hamedrash, they became as familiar to him as his vernacular; while his intercourse with cultivated members of the Ashkenazim community assisted him in his study of the German, which, as his contributions to "Der Orient," &c., will show, he wrote with fluency and elegance. He cultivated the German and French secular literature to an extent, indeed, that not all the orthodox Jewish families would then approve. But his parents combined intelligence with their piety;

---

they did not oppose these studies, and the best authors in all the languages mentioned were placed at his disposal. So with the Jewish philosophico-religious writings. Although the Jewish community of Amsterdam were justly noted for their superior enlightenment; although our student might read the philosophical pages of Arama, Albo, Yehudah Halevi, Maimonides, and others of the Spanish school, without calling forth remark; yet were there many who looked upon the productions of Mendelssohn and his disciples with any thing but favor. But he was too ardent an admirer of this great man's writings to be easily deterred from pursuing their study. At the same time he did not neglect the physical sciences, for which he had acquired a taste while under the instruction of Dr. Benjamin De Sola. On the contrary, he found it absolutely necessary measurably to cultivate them for the proper understanding of the authors he read, and he never would read without comprehending. In late years, when the appearance of such works as the "Bridgewater Treatises" compelled ministers of religion to acquire some knowledge of natural science, he found the value of such a training. Nor did his more serious studies cause him to neglect the acquisition of the accomplishments of life. He became quite a proficient in drawing,* sketching, and music. Of the latter he was all his life passionately fond. Nature had gifted him with a fine ear and most melodious voice, and he composed several very beautiful sacred pieces—a specimen of which we may find in the appendix to a work published by him on the Sephardic Ritual Melodies, which we shall notice hereafter. Mathematics and Astronomy, History and Belles Lettres formed integral parts of his educational course, and so quick and clear was his perception of all he read, so remarkably retentive was his memory, that before he had attained his twentieth year he was regarded as the most learned and gifted young man in the large and intelligent community in which he lived.†

* Beautiful Hebrew caligraphy was at this time highly esteemed as a necessary accomplishment. Some specimens in the possession of the writer, such as an illuminated Omer and portion of a Pentateuch, done by him about 5570, exhibit a proficiency creditable to a *Sopher Mahir*.

† His mother however was not spared to see the fruits of this training; for she changed her earthly cares for the heavenly rest on the 7th April, 21st Nissan, 1817, one year before he entered upon the duties of his future public career.

The ancient and influential congregation Shaar Ashamayim, of London, having decided, in 1818, to appoint a Hazan Sheni, intimation thereof was duly conveyed to the Amsterdam congregation, and the two deemed most competent to fill the office were invited to proceed to London as candidates. The two alumni selected were Solomon Aaron del Canho and David Aaron de Sola; the former, senior with respect to age only, was the warm friend and admirer of his junior fellow-student through life. If we now pause to examine what was the position he was about to assume, what were the requirements of the office he was to fulfil, we shall find that the field he was leaving seemed in every respect more desirable—retrogression rather than advancement appeared to be the prospect. An examination of the *Ascamot** or by-laws, referring to the office and duties of Hazan in this congregation, will sufficiently demonstrate this. Thus we find that, although there may be nominally a Hazan Rishon, or senior Reader, he is only to be considered senior in so far as priority of appointment is concerned,—he has no special duties, no rights or privileges, different from his junior, save, perhaps, a precedence in the performance of divine worship. This duty is to be performed by the two Hazanim in alternate weeks (chap. ix. § 2, p. 35). So also with the solemnization of weddings and births. Section 7, p. 37 shows that the Hazan cannot perform any official act without the permission of the presiding Parnas ; he is to yield obedience to all orders of the Elders of the Mahamad, and any neglect of duty is to be visited with fine or temporary suspension.† Before election, the Hazan is to undergo a probation, which consists in saying prayers in Synagogue as Hazan one whole week, in order

---

* Ascamot, or Laws and Regulations, &c. London, Revised Ed., 5610, 1850.

† The Hazanim, in matters of Synagogue discipline, were, of course, to be considered under the direction of both the Haham and Mahamad (vestry). Thus a letter from the Mahamad chamber, dated 26th July, 1822, directed to the Hazanim, shows that various penalties having been incurred by certain congregators, the Hazanim were directed to guide themselves accordingly, the penalties to remain in force till they received orders to the contrary. The Hazanim were expected to be present at the drawing of the marriage portions given by the Society *Mehil Tsedaca*. See Report 1840, p. 14. The above seem to be the only references made to the office of Hazan.

that all the Yehidim may have opportunity to hear and judge of his capacity and voice. From the above it will be seen that a Reader was required rather than a minister or preacher. But it is proper to remember that the congregation was at this time under the spiritual direction of a Chief Rabbi, whose fame as author, theologian, and scholar was world-wide. It is scarcely necessary to mention the name of Haham Raphael Meldola, himself descended from a family who had given Chief Rabbis and theologians to Italy, France, and Holland uninterruptedly for twelve generations.* Pulpit discourses and supervision of the public schools were, therefore, not expected from the Hazanim,† but devolved upon Haham Meldola, than whom no more zealous friend and promoter of religious education could be found. This is amply shown in an English pamphlet published by him,‡ and in his various Hebrew works, one of which § was partially translated and published by his son and successor, R. David Meldola. Previous to the appointment of Haham Meldola there appears to have been a sorrowful falling off in the religious educational efforts of the congregation, as is shown by the zealous J. Mocatta in his address to the congregation ‖ published in 1803. And although Dr. Meldola introduced many salutary reforms, we yet

---

* See דברי דוד chap. 54, p. 139, and the Biography of R. David Meldola, in the Jewish papers.

† Indeed, not very frequently even from the Haham. The Ascama says: "The Haham shall preach in Synagogue when the Mahamad may require it." This was generally on ש' תשובה 'ש' הגדול and special occasions. The sermons of Haham, and R. David Meldola, chiefly in Spanish, are of marked ability and learning.

‡ Letter to David Abarbanel Lindo, Esq. London, June 19, 5587.

§ דרך אמונה The Way of Faith, &c. London, 5609, S. Meldola & Co.

‖ An address to the congregation of Portuguese Jews, delivered at a meeting of their elders on the examination of the report presented by the committee on the Ecclesiastical State. A. M. 5563. London, Adlard, 1803. He says: "The ecclesiastical state of our nation portends a rapid decline of religion." On p. 8 he refers to the practice of using Spanish and Portuguese in the schools as media of translation, and says: "Hard to tell, we still retain this practice to the exclusion of more significant information   *   *   * they are only proficient in this *ladinaring* and reading."

find that his complaint of the apathy of the people is reiterated by the lay directors of some of the educational institutions,* even when the new Hazan was assuming office. The slight glance we have given will show that the improbability of any extended usefulness or reputation, and the promise of a but limited sphere of action in a community not exempt from a distressing apathy; further a not large stipend increased by the objectionable system of voluntary offerings, tended, unless the distinction of a connection with so respectable and influential a congregation be taken into account, to form a prospect which a young man of respectable status and of more than ordinary talents and acquirements, could scarcely regard as the fullest realization of those soaring aspirations in which youth so much indulge. But it was because he was young, ardent, active, and zealous that he could invest the office with the bright halo of promise; and when advised by his friends to respond to the call, he made the resolve to himself that he would yet widen the narrow sphere he was about to enter, and in elevating his sacred office by a single-minded devotion to the holy cause, benefit his congregation and the Hebrew community at large.† So resolved, he left his home, carrying with him the paternal blessing and the scarcely less prized benediction of his venerable Rabbi, Haham D'Azevedo, who accompanied it with letters of the highest recommendation, nor did he lack the best wishes of his many attached friends.‡

He arrived in England, the 9th of July, 1818, and on the 1st

---

* "It is with deep regret I am compelled to notice that a considerable degree of apathy seems to pervade our ranks." Sketch of a speech delivered by the President of the Spanish and Portuguese Charity Schools, July 1, 1821.

† During his long connection with his congregation, this was always steadily kept in view. In a letter written some thirty years later, he says, that his endeavors have ever been to raise his office, as far as he could, by his personal conduct and unwearied exercise of his talents.

‡ The venerable Chief Rabbi D'Azevedo pathetically laments the separation from him, which he says "is very hard" for him כי קשה עלי פרידתו וכמו שכתב הנשר הגדול רבנו ניסים ז"ל לתלמידו הכופלא יצחק בר ששת כראיתא כתשובות הריב"ש יען כל זה לך לך אכרינן וכו' אולי תמצא חן בעיני בני אדם נם בני איש האנשים האלה שלמים בקהל קדושים וזה שער השמים והיית להם לעינים וכו':

of August (Sabbath Mashé) performed his probationary service
to the satisfaction of a congregation yet vividly impressed with,
and attached to, the ministrations of the popular Hazan, Mordecai
Salom, and then enjoying the able services of the scarcely less
popular Hazan, Isaac Almosnino; but he was elected Hazan on
the 12th of August (10th Menahem) of the same year, an appointment upon which the congregation ever after saw cause to congratulate themselves. On the 20th of May, 1819, he was married
to Rebecca, eldest daughter of the Haham, Dr. Meldola. Born
in Florence, the minister's young bride joined to her native
musical Italian an intimate knowledge of the Spanish and other
continental languages, and, as might have been expected, her
Hebrew and religious training had been specially promoted and
not lost sight of in the acquisition of the various accomplishments
of her sex. Nurtured in that cheerful piety, loftiness of thought,
and thorough culture of heart and mind which the training of
her gifted parents was designed fully to develop, she was a fit-
ting helpmeet for the newly appointed minister. But it was
her unbounded loving devotion to her husband through his life,
her total negation of self for him and for their children, which
caused him ever to regard her as the light of his eyes and his
chief blessing on earth. If ever home was happy and blessed to
the last hour of wedded life, it was theirs.

Having entered on the discharge of his official duties, he continued to perform them with zeal and punctuality. At the same
time, his efforts were directed to the attainment of the English
language and literature with which he had been but slightly acquainted. In this he succeeded most surprisingly, even during
the first year of his appointment, as his correspondence sufficiently shows; and in furtherance of this object he collected
around him an extensive library of standard English works. In
these studies, and in the exercise of the duties of his office, he
employed the first ten years of his appointment, when, having
received intelligence of the serious indisposition of his father, he
prepared to revisit the home of his youth. After the usually
prolonged and comfortless journey of that period, he arrived at
Rotterdam April 3, 1821, where he received alarming tidings of

his father's state. He left the following day for Amsterdam with melancholy forebodings.*

He went to one of his uncles, from whom he learned that his father still lived, but that three of the most eminent physicians who were attending him had declared him incurable. His uncle having duly prepared the invalid, a very affecting interview took place between the father and son. The visit seems to have "had a very beneficial influence on the patient, and quite exhilarated him." He rallied, but died on the 12th of the following June, about two months after his son's return to London. During the stay of the latter in Amsterdam he writes: "The reception I met here from all is most flattering, and I have not a moment to myself." On the Sabbath he was accompanied to the Synagogue, and a seat among the Velhos appropriated to him. He had to devote one entire day to the reception of the immense congregation, among whom came to greet him not a few of his Ashkenazi friends. The same cordial welcome was given him when he revisited Amsterdam (July 29, 1825), the London Synagogue then undergoing repairs, and not re-opening for public service till the 9th of September of the same year.†

In 1829 appeared his first published work, "The Blessings," with an introductory essay on Thanksgiving.‡ Laying down the

---

* He writes: "I tremble at every footstep I take towards home; for God knows what I shall find there." On his arrival at Amsterdam he writes: "I reached here at six o'clock in the morning. I cannot possibly describe to you with what feelings I again entered my native city, not daring to enter our house abruptly, and not knowing whether I should embrace my father alive or be obliged to bewail him. You may suppose what I felt when I reached our door where I stood like one enchanted, and as if I would have inquired from the stones of the house the situation of my father. Being early in the morning, few people were yet stirring, and of these I was afraid to inquire, expecting to hear the worst."

* Though divine service was performed in the smaller buildings of the congregation.

† סדר ברכות "The Blessings;" or, expressions of praise and thanksgiving said by Israelites on various occasions, with an interlineary translation, accompanied with an explication of their source, the precepts and דינים (regulations) attached to them, and explanatory notes. To which is prefixed an introductory essay on the nature and duty of thanksgiving." London, Wertheimer, Barnet & Soloman, 5590–1829. 8vo.

rule that it is "desirable to collect a variety of useful matter
within a small compass, and to divest it of the austere garb of a
professed book of instruction without, at the same time, detract-
ing from its usefulness," he designed the work to be "a book of
religious information as well as a manual of private devotion."
He states, in a lucid manner, the origin of the various precepts,
explains the same, and adds much useful matter for those unable
to consult the original Hebrew. The interlinear system of translation is adopted in the text in order to give some "insight into
the construction and idiom of the Hebrew, and to incite to the
study of those rules of grammar by which a competent knowledge
of the sacred language might be obtained."   The origin of the
subject and plan of the work, he gratefully mentions, originated
with Moses Montefiore, Esq., (afterwards Sir Moses Montefiore),
to whom he was afterwards no less indebted for the generous
support he gave to his published works than for countless proofs
of a warm an enduring friendship.*

The Essay on Thanksgiving renders this work particularly
valuable. It is written in that terse, vigorous style which he
always retained, and at once called the attention of the anglo-
Jewish community to him, and, we believe, gave no small impetus
to the organization חברת אור תורה, when he associated with Dr.
Joshua van Oven, Michael Josephs, Selig Newman, and others,
in maintaining this Hebra as an adult school. We have before us
a communication to him, dated March 7, 1830, from the manag-
ing committee, who, being "desirous of continuing the delivery
of religious and instructive lectures on Saturdays at the Jews'
Free School, and quite assured of his excellent talent for that
purpose, request the favor of his services for 20th March."

---

* They were both doubtlessly anxious to introduce something that should
usefully substitute the old system of *ladinaring;* and although Hannaniah
Bolaffey had published one part or number of his מורה התהלות, or "Extracts
from the Prayers," with an interlinear translation, yet he did not proceed
with his work. Mr. B. was author of a very good Hebrew grammar and
primer, was a good linguist and Hebrew writer, and was for some time
teacher at Eton College, and Hebrew master of the Sephardim schools in
London.

The same year his co-operation was solicited by, and given to, "The Society for the Cultivation of the Hebrew Language and Literature," his co-laborers being Michael Josephs,* Dr. Van Oven,† Arthur Lumley Davids,‡ Marris Jacob Raphall,§ Selig Newman,|| and others. The present venerable Sampson Samuel was secretary of the society. His services were rewarded by the warm acknowledgments of the committee, and a solicitation "for the repetition of his favors, the continuance of which would enable the society to look forward to the future with hope and confidence." His subject was "Sacred Biography as connected with Hebrew Literature," on which he gave three lectures, the continuation being in the following session (Oct. 31), all of which were duly acknowledged in very flattering terms. His success in this department seems to have determined some intelligent members of his congregation—among whom were the Mahamad or vestry—to realize their wish for the introduction of occasional English discourses in the Synagogue. On his assenting to their wish, the first English sermon ever heard within the walls of the ancient Portuguese Synagogue in London was delivered by him on Sabbath Hagadol, 12th Nissan, 5591, (26th March, 1831,) before a large and admiring audience. As religious discourses had been hitherto of very unfrequent occurrence, and invariably delivered in the Spanish or Portuguese languages, the preacher found himself in a more than ordinary

---

* Author of the English-Hebrew Lexicon, &c. He lectured on the book of Job.

† Author of the Manual of Judaism, &c. He was one of the original projectors and founders of the Jews' Free School.

‡ Author of the Turkish Grammar, &c. His lecture was on the Philosophy of the Jews. Published in 1833, early after his death.

§ Here commenced his intimacy with the learned Raphall, his subsequent co-laborer. Dr. Raphall then gave one lecture on Hebrew Poetry, which we believe afterwards grew out to that course to which so many have listened. Mr. De Sola cordially compliments him in his own lecture.

|| Author of Emendations of the Scriptures, Hebrew Grammar, Lexicon, Challenge Accepted, &c.

C

embarrassing position. We will quote from his introduction to
the printed discourse,* his own description of its origin :—

"The gentlemen elders of the congregation, impressed with
these truths (just referred to by him), and ever ready to promote
the spiritual improvement of the congregation, finding that,
owing to the change of times and circumstances, the religious
instruction hitherto given in the Synagogue in the Spanish language had ceased to be useful, since that language is at the
present day no longer understood by the greater portion of those
members of the congregation who are natives of this country,
resolved that in future sermons in the English language should
be delivered, in order to afford the congregation religious instruction in the only way it could prove useful. Some gentlemen of that body did me the honor to declare their opinion that
they considered me fit to execute their laudable intention ; and
although I was deeply impressed with the arduousness of the
task required of me, and justly diffident of any capacity to do it
justice, yet hoping that the purity of my intention, and the

---

* A Sermon on the Excellence of the Holy Law, and the Necessity and
Importance of Religious Instruction. London, H. Barnett and M. Solomon,
1831. This sermon and the auspicious occasion called forth the following beautifully written eulogy of the preacher, by an anonymous hand. We believe
it was the production of his esteemed friend, the venerable Michael Josephs :

לכבוד איש משכיל ויקר רוח חזן דוד די כולה יצו' שלום וישע : נקרה נקרתי
בתוך הבאים אשר התאספו בשבת הגדול יום אשר הבאת את פרי ארשך ובשרת צדק
בשפת ארצנו שמיעתי רבריך כי ניעמו בם הרוית נפש שקקה לשמיע מוסר השכל בלשון
למורים וייען כי אף אנכי טעבתי כמתק מלין והיו לי לעינים אמרתי אגישה לך את ברכתי
מנחת אהבה ותורה והיתה לך לכזכרת מאת אהבך איש בריטאני ושמו פלאי :

אחיך יורוך ישרון יהללך
כי הנדלת יעל שביעך אמרותיך
יעת כי צדק בשרת במקהלות
לקח טוב נתת הלכת בנרולות
הן ברוח בינה ובשפתי דיעת
ניעם הטפת יעלי אזן שמיעת
בכחנה היעכרים חדשות השמיעת
נפתלה אחי נפתלה—ויכלת :

הקבצו בני ייעקב ושמיעו נאוכו
נאם הנבר הכרבר בלשון יעכו :

beauty and holiness inherent in the subject on which I was to treat, might induce an indulgent audience of my brethren to look leniently upon the imperfections of a first attempt, joined to the desire of marking, by a prompt obedience, my sense of the honor conferred on me by their request, I was induced to make an effort to surmount all difficulties; and the result was that I found I had not miscalculated upon the forbearance and indulgence of my brethren, since my attempt was honored with their approbation." On page 1 we are made acquainted with the feelings which, when standing up to speak to the people, "agitated and almost overpowered" him. He asks that due allowance should be made for them, because of the peculiar difficulties attending his undertaking, the honor and perhaps also the boldness of raising his feeble voice within those holy walls which had so often resounded with the eloquence of great, wise, and pious men, to address an audience so numerous and well informed as he then felt honored in behaloing. The nature of the subject on which he was to speak, diffidence of his qualifications to do it justice, dread of criticism of all kinds, the apprehension of the imputation of vain presumption, together with the many other difficulties inseparable from a first attempt—all these were sufficient to appal even the stoutest heart, and claim indulgence "in the prosecution of his new career—new not only to me but in some degree also to yourselves, this being the first day on which a sermon was ever pronounced within this holy place in the language of this country."

His next published sermon * (and it is only to his published sermons that we shall now refer, giving a list of those in MS. hereafter) was on the "Consolation of Jerusalem," delivered on Sabbath Nahamu (Menahem 11, 5693—July 27, 1833). This was just before those dark days when many a family in England needed consolation, his own not excepted; for on his return in August from Amsterdam, where he had piously proceeded to visit his parents' graves (קבר אבות), he received the overwhelming intelligence that one of his sons had been snatched from him after a few hours' illness only by Asiatic cholera, then devastat-

---

* "The Consolation of Jerusalem," a sermon &c., printed by the express desire of the gentlemen of the Mahamad. London, Wertheimer, 5594.

ing London.   Only the preceding year he had followed to the
grave an infant son.   His pious resignation, however, enabled
him to recover from what was a very terrible shock to him.   His
public duties also tended to engage him from his private griefs;
and when Dr. Raphall started his "Hebrew Review," in 1834,
he took a lively interest in its success, and contributed some
literary assistance.   One article in volume iii. (p. 381, et seq.)
was called forth from his observing in Peter Beer's *Geschichte
aller Sekten der Juden*, his partiality for the Caraites, and his
scarcely disguised hostility to the Talmud, which led him to
represent Caraitism in a much better light than is conformable
with truth.   His pulpit duties also claimed much of his attention.   He was sought now to make English discourses a permanent institution.   Thus the Mahamad resolved that at least once
a month discourses should be delivered by Hazan De Sola during
the year 5595 (1835), and a notice to that effect was duly published and sent to the members.   The twelve sermons were delivered in due course.

The same year appeared his proposals for a new Translation
of the Portuguese Prayers.   In a prospectus of four octavo pages,
he lays down four main rules for his guidance in translation, and
to which he, in fact, strictly adheres in his work.   The Hebrew
text was most scrupulously collated and revised from the best continental editions, such as Athias, Silva Mendes, Rodrigues Mendes, Templo, Heidenheim, &c., and the important particular of
a clear and perfect vowel punctuation rigidly attended to.   In
the English translation, that of David Levi was taken as a basis;
but this was very generally departed from, when the author's
study of the original, aided by a careful comparison with Haham
Nietto in Spanish, Fiorentino and Ottolenghi in Italian, Ventura
in French, Euchel and Friedlander in German, and other continental translators, rendered it desirable.   D. Levi was unable
to avail himself of the advantages of these translations, and, as
truly stated in this prospectus, was "very unsuccessful in trans-
fusing the spirit and beauty of the original,"—though Levi's
work (5549–1789), as cordially admitted, was "the first deserv-
ing the name of a translation,"—the incompetent efforts of Gam-
liel ben Pedaazur and A. Alexander not meriting notice but as

first attempts. The former editions being out of print, it was deemed a proper opportunity to prevent defective editions being multiplied by mercenary booksellers;* and he was induced to undertake the task, urged thereto by many gentlemen of zeal, taste, and ability, but chiefly by Sir Moses Montefiore, who very munificently supported this, as he did his previous and subsequent publications. The "additional matter" of this edition is stated under ten heads, one of which is the valuable tabular matter with which this edition was enriched.

The work † on its appearance was received with the utmost satisfaction and approval on the part of his congregation, the universal opinion being that expressed by one of the leading members, that "it conferred infinite credit on him and lasting obligation on the part of the community." It received the warmest laudations also of the German-Jewish press (there was then no Jewish periodical in England). The *Algemeine Zeitung des Judenthums* (Beiblatt, 2 J. No. 13) devotes five of its quarto columns, and again two columns (April 30, 1839), to a review of the whole work, "which," writes the editor, "has made on us one of the most agreeable impressions." Farther, he says: "That in England the Portuguese community should become sensible of the want of a good translation of their liturgy is not be wondered at, as they have been so deficient in this respect. It is pleasing, then, to see that this undertaking has fallen into the hands of Mr. De Sola, and that it has obtained so much support. * * A number of names of old and illustrious families appear among them, and Jamaica, United States, Sydney, Montreal, &c., have received their copies. * * * The characteristics of Mr. De Sola's translation are clearness and perspicuity. * * * In taking this laborious task on himself, Mr. De Sola has rendered himself highly meritorious to the English-Portuguese Synagogue, and its results will doubtless prove beneficial to that community.

---

* See the preface.

† Forms of Prayer according to the customs of the Spanish and Portuguese Jews, with an English Translation. To which are added tables, forming a complete Hebrew Almanac, from A. M. 5596–1836, till the year 5646–1886. London, 5596–1836, J. Wertheimer. An edition of the Daily Prayers, all Hebrew, was published in the same year.

The author, in a beautifully written preface of sixteen pages to volume one, offers first, some thoughts on prayer in general, then a short history of our liturgy, and treats finally of the various translations of the prayers for the Spanish and Portuguese Jews. * * * Of the *Adon Olam* he has given a metrical translation."

Without entering into a full examination of this work, we may add to what the German reviewer has stated, that one feature presented is the valuable notes with which it is interspersed, both at the foot of the pages and in supplemental form. The tabular matter at the end of the first volume, forming an almanac for fifty years, exhibits, of course, a close intimacy with the Jewish calendar system, and was itself a labor of no slight character. We will also not dwell upon the extensive intimacy with Rabbinical literature which his rendering of the Piyutim for Kippur, Roshashana, and the Festivals indicate; we refer only to the laudatory terms in which the German reviewer speaks of his translation of the *Keter Malchuth* of R. S. ben Gabirol in the third volume.* To this translation he added an introduction, in which, after a brief notice of the author and design of the poem, he points out the difference between the Copernican and Ptolemaic systems, on which latter the astronomical references of the poem are based, adding an astronomical table for the purpose of comparing and rectifying modern calculations and those received in the days of Gabirol. Dr. S. I. Mulder, in Amsterdam, printed on his model an edition of the Daily Prayers in Dutch in the same year, and refers in most complimentary terms to his London prototype, and copies all the tables. But though a close copy, even in mechanical execution, yet it is in every respect inferior, the London edition still remaining the most beautiful specimen of Hebrew printing extant, and only equalled by the second edition, which the translator subsequently undertook of the same work. Both Hebrew and English type were new. The Hebrew was cut expressly for the work by the celebrated firm of Messrs. Alexander Wilson & Sons, Glasgow, and the matrices were copied from the letter of Athias, as being the best specimen

---

* The erudite Dukes also refers to his translation of this poem. J. Chr., Vol. v. No. 31.

of printed Hebrew attainable. It has now almost entirely super-
seded all other fonts in England. The printing of the work
reflected the highest credit on the office of Wertheimer, and was
chiefly performed by Messrs. Samuel Meldola and Coppe Green.

This work, though of great magnitude, did not distract his
attention from his newly imposed pulpit duties; and accordingly
we find, that on 26th Kislev, 5597, (1837,) the elders passed a
resolution, conveyed to him by Hananel De Castro, Esq., the
President, assuring him of "their thanks and entire approbation
of the very able manner in which he had delivered his sermons
during the past and preceding years."

During the outbreak of the Druses in Safet, &c., in 1838, he was
employed in translating correspondence, reports, &c., affecting
the Israelites of the Holy Land. This year was also an eventful
one for the Hebrew community in England. A growing desire
for change in the Synagogue worship, and perhaps also for cere-
monial observances, had been for some time manifest on the part
of many leading members of both Sephardim and Ashkenazim.
A choir was introduced, first in the Portuguese and afterwards
in the German Synagogue, but not with general approval. Sus-
picious of the length to which the reform leaders desired to go,
a large conservative party had determined to oppose all conces-
sions to what they deemed mere clamor; and this produced an
antagonism which resulted in the formation of the Burton Street
congregation. We have before us a very complete report of a
meeting of the Yehidim, held at the Mahamad Chamber, in
Heshvan, 1838, being the notes taken by Hazan De Sola, who
was present as a Yahid of the congregation. It exhibits the
prevalence of an unfortunate spirit of contention from which no
good result could possibly follow. At this meeting, a proposi-
tion was made for the appointment of a committee, in which the
Hazanim were to be included, " to inquire into the propriety of
altering or curtailing the prayers, and to supply more regular
religious instruction." The stormy discussion which arose there-
upon was but the prelude to others of a more violent character;
and organizations were formed out of the meetings on both sides.
One of these called שכרי משכרת הקרש, or "Society for supporting
and upholding the Jewish religion as handed down to us by our

ancestors, and for preventing innovations or alterations in any of its recognised forms and customs, unless sanctioned by properly constituted religious authorities," was formed almost immediately after the meeting above mentioned, and its founders issued a circular inviting co-operation on 26th Heshvan, (14th November) 1838. This agitation originated Mr. De Sola's next literary work, the translation into English of eighteen treatises of the Mishnah. Some three years after the completion of the MS., Mr. Benjamin Elkin, a zealous member of the Burton Street congregation, put the work to press,* and, without the knowledge or consent of the translator,† added an anonymously written preface, and announced the publication of the work in the *Times* of 23d December, 1842. This preface states the origin of the work to be in consequence of the discussions at the Vestry Board of the Sephardim, when the reform party "urged the necessity of being supplied with an English translation of the Mishnah from persons of their own faith. In consequence of this application, the meeting passed a resolution authorizing the Rev. · D. A. De Sola to translate the Mishnah. Mr. De Sola having been empowered to call in a coadjutor made choice of the Rev. M. J. Raphall." Mr. Elkin, we find, had been no party to the articles of agreement drawn up between the translators and the original projectors of the work. Of the latter, only two names, Moses Mocatta and Horatio J. Montefiore, appear. Upon the publication of the advertisement, the translators formally repudiated (by advertisement in the *Times* of 29th) all connection with the work, " which they had not seen since they completed the translation some three years ago, and, consequently, had not been revised or prepared by them for publication." They add, "that the prospectus and preface were not written by them, and that they were in every way unconnected with the publication of the work."

---

* משניות י"ח מכבתות ששה סדרי משנה, " Eighteen Treatises of the Mishnah, translated by the Rev. D. A. De Sola and the Rev. M. J. Raphall." London, Sherwood, Gilbert & Piper, 1842.

† And also without the knowledge of the projectors of, and parties to, the translation, as communications from these to Mr. De Sola clearly show.

During the six days intervening the two advertisements, we find from a formal disclaimer sent to the Jewish press,* that the translators say, " We procured the work, and find from the cursory view we have given to it that, as our translation was hurried through the press without our knowledge, it has not undergone that revision and correction which even the most carefully executed work requires, and was brought under the public eye with all its imperfections.   *   *   *   *   But when we see that the attempt is made, under the sanction of our names, to foist on the public a spurious preface—spurious, because not written by us, or even with our knowledge, and expressing sentiments we do not entertain, we do not stay to examine whether this unfair proceeding had for its object to ruin us in public estimation, or simply to obtain for the anti-Judaic principles expressed in the preface such weight as our names might be supposed to impart to them." " The anti-Judaic principles above referred to," adds the editor, " we understand to include a covert attempt to bring the Mishnah into contempt as well as the oral law which it contains."† It were needless to review the controversy which arose on this subject. Mr. Elkin issued a pamphlet of thirty pages,‡ in which he endeavored to show that no discourtesy was intended the translators, though in perusing this pamphlet after so long a lapse of time, one cannot but be surprised how a gentleman, who in his day, was so generally and deservedly respected, should have allowed his zeal to outrun his discretion and sense of strict justice.§

In 1840, Mr. De Sola issued a prospectus of a new edition of the Sacred Scriptures, with notes critical and explanatory. His

---

* " Voice of Jacob," No. 37, January 6, 1843.

† The editor remarks, " We know the preface was ascribed to them by cursory readers."

‡ Letters addressed to the editor of the " Voice of Jacob," &c., by the writer of the preface to the lately published Mishnah. London, J. Wertheimer, 1843.

§ An ostensible publisher advertised subsequently in the Jewish papers that the Rev. translators were not connected with the publication. The preface has an italicised passage referring to the *expressive* silence of Scripture with reference to an oral law.

D

literary co-laborer was again Dr. Raphall, while the correction of the Hebrew text and the publishing department was entrusted chiefly to Mr. I. L. Lindenthal, Secretary of the new Synagogue. The prospectus, embracing a brief history of former translations, was in itself a valuable literary production, and was republished in Germany by Dr. Fürst in his *Orient*, (No. 52, December 26, 1840), when welcoming the publication. We will only quote from this prospectus some details, in order to show the plan of the work, which was executed in strict conformity therewith.

" The Hebrew text will be printed with the most scrupulous attention to correctness in every particular, and will be carefully collated with all the acknowledged authorities.   In the English translation we will endeavor to combine elegance with perspecuity, and a strict adherence to the literal meaning of the text. Our model in this respect will be Mendelssohn's version, and like him, we shall carefully avail ourselves of the Targumim, and of the various commentaries and translations.   Respecting the notes, it is intended, in order to assist the reader without distracting his attention, to give explanatory notes at the bottom of each page, and at the end of each weekly section to append notes illustrating the following subjects :—1. Explanations of the precepts as they respectively occur in each section, particularly of those in use at present.   2. Critical and grammatical investigations, reconciling apparent contradictions, solving questions, and removing difficulties that present themselves in the text. 3. Moral reflections and inferences to be deduced from the events related in each weekly section, which will, in some degree, supply the want of religious instruction in our Synagogues. 4. Sacred geography, geology, and natural history of the Bible, manners and customs of the East, &c.   Under this head will be collected the best of all that has appeared in modern publications on these subjects—travels in the Holy Land, together with whatever information ancient writers have bequeathed to us. The whole of the notes will be selected from an immense variety of sources and authorities, in all languages, both ancient and modern."

The plan of the work received the formal approval of the Rev.

Dr. Meldola, Chief Rabbi of the Portuguese,* and of the Rev. Dr. Solomon Hirschel, Chief Rabbi of the German congregation. Its importance was duly recognised by the Jewish press, and regarded as a pleasing sign of the times.† Its first number, which appeared in September, 1841, created a profound sensation also in Christian literary circles, " it being the first work of the kind ever issued in England by learned Jews ;" and the translators were overwhelmed with letters of congratulation from all classes! High dignitaries of the church showed their interest in the undertaking,, though perhaps no one was more deeply interested in its progress than the Rev. George Becket, a learned and amiable divine and cordial friend of Jewish emancipation. The completion of the first volume‡ (consisting of seven hundred and ten pages 8vo.) elicited the same cordial commendations of the press.§ It was a matter of deep regret to all that the publication was not farther continued. The chief causes of its discontinuance we believe to have been the irregularity of those entrusted with its publication, and the unwillingness of Mr. De Sola to continue so grave a literary undertaking by himself when Dr. Raphall had removed to the pastoral charge of the Birmingham congregation, though we find that Mr. Lin-

---

* This revered Rabbi writes in a periodical of which he was co-editor (*Jewish Chronicle*, 1st Series, No. 11, January 28. 1842) : " It will be to this generation of Israelites the most valuable book they can possess. The choicest passages have been culled by master hands from our most eminent commentators, and translated into English, so that the great difficulty to the perfect understanding of the holy law is removed.

† See " Voice of Jacob," No. 1, an article by the erudite Theodores in No. 2, and a review in No. 3, &c.

‡ כפר תורת ה' The Sacred Scriptures, in Hebrew and English; a new translation, with notes critical and explanatory, &c., vol. 1, Genesis. London, Bagster, 1844.

§ *Jewish Chronicle*, January 3, 1845.—Even at the Antipodes the same note was heard. A Christian writer in Sydney adopts the opinion of another London Christian critic, that "the book is one of extraordinary learning," and "the result will open up sources of interest and inquiry for readers of every faith." "Such," he adds, "is the natural effect of true learning. It does not labor to become exclusive and sectarian." See *Australian*, June 2, 1842, and the Sydney " Voice of Jacob," June 24, 1842.

denthal is said* to have asserted that "it was not continued for the want of that support which such a work had a right to expect." The list of contents shows the work to have been pretty equally divided between Messrs. De Sola and Raphall, one section only having been translated and annotated by Mr. Lindenthal. In 5603 (1843) they issued another edition of Genesis,† being the English translation without the Hebrew text and notes, the only difference between these two versions being, that in the larger work they give the Scriptural names in accordance with the orthography of the Hebrew text, and in the second they retain the ordinary mode of spelling these names.

While engaged in a work of so grave a character, his literary aid was sought and cheerfully rendered to an effort originating with the late excellent and amiable Charlotte Montefiore, to supply the humble classes of Israelites with interesting and instructive reading. The pious design of this lamented lady was carried out in conjunction with her sister and Mr. De Sola, and the "Cheap Jewish Library" appeared. The first volume consisted of seven moral and religious tales, or as in the "Evenings in Judea," in the second volume, useful information is conveyed in the form of a dialogue on the Geography of Palestine, History and Antiquities of the Jews, &c. Of the design of the work, the authoress says: "Amongst the many means that have hitherto been employed to inculcate religious truths and principles of morality, none have proved more efficient than the publication of tracts in the form of tales conveying instruction and entertainment.‡ The position of the worthy authoress enabled her to publish them at a pecuniary loss, a nominal price having been put upon each number, while it was announced at the same time, that they might be obtained for the poor by application to

---

* See letters of N. H. Solomon, S. C., &c., in the *Jewish Chronicle*, December, 1852. This periodical frequently copied the notes of the work. Some letters on the Egyptian names occurring in the Scriptures from Dr. Loewe to Rev. D. A. De Sola were not published. See preface.

† The Sacred Scriptures; translated from the original Hebrew, &c. London,   , 5603.

‡ Several of the tales were reprinted in America, as soon as they appeared, by the Jewish Publication Society of Philadelphia. They were also republished by several periodicals.

the Rev. D. A. De Sola, who, in a letter to a friend, gives the following account of their publication:

* * * "Therefore they essayed what good could be done by the publication of moral tracts in the attractive garb of tales for Jewish readers. They commenced by printing two hundred and fifty copies of each of the four first tales, which were published at one penny, or, when they exceeded two sheets, at two pence each. It is not necessary to state to any one acquainted with printing, that this was tantamount to giving them away. But these ladies wisely judged, that what was given away was either looked upon with suspicion or neglected; whereas, if the class for which it was intended were to make the sacrifice of even a penny to buy it, it would show that they appreciated it, and that they had a desire for useful literature. They had the gratification to see that the said small impression was soon exhausted, and another edition of five hundred (though at an additional sacrifice) was issued by them. For the good of their humbler brethren these ladies continue to devote their talents, time, and means. Their strict incognito prevents their receiving the thanks of their brethren, being content 'to do good by stealth, and blush to find it fame.' * * * As it was necessary that some one should attend to the publication, I was honored with their confidence, and willingly undertook the pleasing task of promoting their good intentions."

This confidence was duly respected, and the incognito of the authoress always maintained on his part. It may be permitted us here, however, now that both authoress and editor have been removed from their earthly labors, to show by some extracts from the correspondence—written *currente calamo*—of this most worthy daughter of Israel with Mr. De Sola, how warmly she felt and how much she intended to do had she been spared for her people, more especially for that humbler class, in whom all her thoughts and sympathies seemed to be centered, notwithstanding the many seductions of her exalted position and immense wealth. She writes to Mr. De Sola thus:

"From what I had heard of your general kindness, I had expected that my project would come in for a share of it; but I never could have anticipated that you would take so deep an interest in its success, and be willing to devote so much time to the furtherance of it. Nothing could have given me so much courage to proceed as the knowledge of having some one to assist me, who, like yourself, has so intimate an acquaintance with Jewish character, manners, and religion. Pray accept my sincerest thanks for what you have said upon the subject, and for what you have offered to do. You have quite excited my curiosity about the additional things you wish my 'Letter to the Jews' to contain, and shall feel greatly obliged if you will gratify it as soon as possible. * * * I fear I am exceedingly deficient as regards the habits and prejudices of the Jews of the working class. This may affect all I write, weakening its utility and depriving it of a character of reality which is certainly one of the greatest charms of such works. By an earnest study of the Bible I may learn all what the Jews *ought to be*, and, derived from that sacred source, I trust my delineations of good may always be correct. To trace what they are requires a different study. I must be indebted to you if I do so at all faithfully. I intend to make it a personal study; but this will demand time. Upon such points of religion as can hardly be treated in tales, I purpose writing little essays or discourses. As soon as any are completed, they shall be forwarded to you for your criticism or approval; but whatever opinions they may give rise to, I hope you will always have the kindness to tell me quite frankly. I am confident that I shall be always very grateful for your suggestions, which will be to me of great utility, and contribute materially to the success of my undertaking. * * * In the approval of Mrs. De Sola and your daughters of 'Rachel Levi,' I have a most agreeable guarantee of success, which, as you may suppose, has been a matter of great doubt and anxiety to me. Will you be good enough to say to them that the author heard with the greatest pleasure that they took some interest in the story of the orphan, and that the writer hopes their good wishes will attend Rachel's entrance into the world. * * * I ought to apologize for taking up so much of your time, and accepting your kind offer of devoting still more to my service. I trust it may not be to my service alone, but, with the Almighty's blessing, prove a lasting benefit to many of our humble brethren. In this case you will need no thanks of mine, being far more fully repaid by the good you will have effected." On another occasion she writes Mr. De Sola: "All the information I may have, all the energy and perseverance that has been bestowed upon me, I have long wished to consecrate to the religious good of our poor brethren. I must, I know, expect to meet with difficulties; but these I hope eventually, by patience and perseverance, to overcome. And I am likewise prepared to find it a losing concern, in one sense of the word; but if it should be of real utility to but even a very few, I shall be amply repaid. My task must remain incomplete, unless you give me the benefit of your superior abilities. With another undertaking on hand, this I feel is requesting a service I can never hope adequately to return; but I solicit it with confidence, as I ask it for the welfare of those to whose interests you have always devoted yourself." She was very desirous that Mr. De Sola should establish a Jewish periodical, and says: "I should be really delighted if in some little way I could promote the success of an undertaking likely to be productive of so extended an utility, besides the pleasure it would give me to be able to do any thing that would be agreeable to one to whom I am so much indebted. I have a friend who writes beautifully, and who would be willing to add some contributions."

Mr. De Sola was very desirous that Grace Aguilar, his friend and pupil,[*] in whom he ever took a paternal interest, should contribute to the "Cheap Jewish Library," and with the ready consent and the encouragement of the amiable editress, Miss Aguilar wrote the "Perez Family," which duly appeared in the series. In a communication to Mr. De Sola on this subject, Miss Aguilar says:

"But in a Christian country we should rather enlarge on the tenets of our faith, not perhaps so much for our own people as to do away with some of the mistaken notions regarding it adopted by other creeds. This is my simple opinion, which I hope you will not consider too free." With reference to the Perez Family,

---

[*] She was then studying Hebrew under Mr. De Sola, and was always accustomed to guide herself very much by his advice, and to apply to him for information in all cases of doubt. She showed her respect for him and appreciation of his writings by frequently quoting from them in her works. See "Spirit of Judaism," "Women of Israel," &c.

she writes on another occasion : "The whole tale was written while sickening for and recovering from a severe illness. * * I still indulge the hope, however fallacious, of one day seeing my writings more known than they are now."

Referring to this effort of Miss Aguilar, the amiable editress writes Mr. De Sola :

"I cannot tell you how much pleasure it gives me to have seen something by one of our co-religionists that is so good as Miss A.'s story. I sincerely congratulate her upon having the means of raising some time, by her talent, the opinion that is entertained of Jewish intellectual abilities. It is quite a satisfaction to think that a Jew may become celebrated for something else than their wealth and their talent on the stock exchange. For this alone it would be worth Miss Aguilar's while to devote her energy, time, and talents to the cultivation of her intellectual powers. * * * If I did not make any allusions to the commendations Miss Aguilar bestowed, it was not from indifference to them, but because agreeable truths are always known to be · more acceptable, and to me, who am still very anxious as to the probable success of my arduous undertaking, particularly so."

We cannot say that the wealthy classes of our English co-religionists followed the patriotic example of our worthy authoress * and her respected sister, Lady Rothschild, who assisted her. One honorable exception to this remark should be made. Mr. Haim Guedallah published his "Sabbath Leaves,"† containing sermons of our most esteemed divines (among them he announces Rev. D. A. De Sola); but after publishing some five numbers, he was compelled to relinquish it owing to the extreme apathy of the people.

---

* This pious and excellent woman died July 2, 1854. In an obituary written on what was every where deemed a national loss, the writer says : "In an afflicted body conversant with him, the deceased harbored a mind overflowing with affection to its kind, and constantly solicitous to relieve its miseries. She to whom physical exertion was not easy, she who had been reared in all the luxuries of life, who could only have known misery from hearsay, she not only did not shrink back from visiting in person the dingy lanes and dismal hovels where wretchedness, sickness, and its concomitant evils revelled, but delighted to appear as an angel of mercy in the abodes of poverty.—*Heb. Observer*, July 7, 1854.

† "Sabbath Leaves," adapted for the use of Jewish families, to be read on Sabbaths, &c.   London, April, 1845.

On the return of Sir Moses Montefiore and his worthy lady from their patriotic journey to the East in behalf of the persecuted Jews of Damascus, a solemn service was held in the Portuguese Synagogue on the 8th of March, 1841, and the extensive edifice was crowded to its utmost capacity by the elite of the Jewish community, besides many eminent Christians.* On this occasion he was selected to preach,† and while he duly dwelt on the topic appropriate to the occasion, he did not fail to refer to the example of civil and religious liberty shown by the Sultan, and the claims Israel as a people had thereto—a topic which, when the report of his sermon appeared in the London press, was duly taken by them as a hint that England "should go and do so likewise," and improved by the liberal portion of the press for the special behoof of those who still persistently opposed Jewish emancipation. That emancipation was a subject in which he had intense interest is sufficiently demonstrated by his writings and correspondence; though he had too high a sense of the dignity of his office to allow himself to appear in public as a political orator. In connection with a few friends, he was instrumental, during the following year (1842), in organizing an "Association for the promotion of Jewish Literature." We quote the following exposition of the design:

"It would be supererogatory to dilate on the benefits to be derived from the promotion of Jewish literature by a general circulation of the valuable works which daily issue from various presses without limitation of language, but which, owing to several circumstances, it is but in the power of a few to obtain. The Rev. D. A. De Sola, Mr. Lindenthal, and Dr. Benisch have been elected a provisional committee," &c. And again,‡ "The attention which is now forced upon Jews throughout the civilized world is well known. It is owing to this attention that eminent men are constantly laying down in highly valuable pub-

---

* In the splendid piece of plate presented as a testimonial to Sir Moses, he had the honor, in company with his colleague, to be represented, as they stood near Sir Moses when the latter repeated the *Agomel*. ("Voice of Jacob," vol. ii. p. 18.)

† The "Orient," (25th May, 1841,) refers in laudatory terms to this discourse.

‡ "Voice of Jacob," vol. ii. Nos. 32 and 34.

E

lications the result of their researches and reflections on Israel. It is clear that Israel itself, the object of this attention, should be acquainted with what is said of it."

This organization was not more permanent than the "Jews and General Literary and Scientific Institution," at Sussex Hall, subsequently started under the presidency of Hananel De Castro, Esq. In this he also took great interest from its commencement. Thus we find him assisting at the opening of the lecture season, and on many other occasions; and although his multifarious duties prevented his giving the more active assistance he desired, yet he was represented in the committee of management by his son, and through him made many useful suggestions, assisting the classes with books, &c. In the early part of the year 1843, his colleague, the Rev. Isaac Almosnino was attacked with a very painful malady which incapacitated him from the performance of his duties, and which terminated fatally on Friday, 16th Tamooz, (14th July) of the same year. The decease of Hazan Almosnino was a source of much grief to him, and on him devolved the performance of the last sad rites. "The reverend colleague of the departed, (Mr. De Sola,) who read the prayers, was deeply affected," writes the *Jewish Reporter*.* Indeed he was losing the daily companion of a quarter of a century, and one whom he had always regarded and treated with respectful consideration and warm friendship. His official duties were, therefore, now considerably increased; and as the Synagogue was to be re-opened, after a thorough repair, on Friday, 22d September,† the training of a choir, in conjunction with Mr. Saqui, was super-added to his other duties. During these repairs, the regular services were continued in the Mahamad and Medras buildings, and until the appointment of the Rev. David Piza, he was assisted by Mr. Judah Mudahi, and his son, Abraham. On the 12th May, 1844, he had the pleasure of seeing realized a project in which he was much interested,—the opening of an infant school for the children of the congregation, erected at the cost of Mrs. Lara. On this occasion "he addressed the children a suitable admoni-

---

* "Voice of Jacob," vol. ii., No. 51.

† "The Voice of Jacob," vol. iii., No. 56, contains an account of this "impressive ceremony."

tion and exhortation, which was conceived in a spirit worthy of the occasion, as we are still better able to affirm from a more deliberate perusal."*

In this year Mr. Abraham Mendes, of Kingston, Jamaica, arrived in England, with the design of completing his Hebrew and theological studies under Mr. De Sola. Mr. Mendes was chiefly urged to this step by his friends from the fact that three Englishmen who had gone to the West Indies to fill the ministerial office had successively died of the yellow fever. Mr. Mendes, in conjunction with his fellow-student, Abraham De Sola, pursued his theological course under Mr De Sola, until the autumn of the year 1846, when he was appointed minister of Kingston, Jamaica; and Abraham De Sola was appointed at the same time to the ministry of Montreal, Canada. And if the public labors of these, his loving disciples, have been, or shall hereafter be, at all instrumental in promoting the spiritual weal of their brethren, or disabusing the Gentile mind of the erroneous notions it is wont to entertain of Jews and Judaism, to his patient, learned teachings, to his valuable advice, above all, to his excellent practical example, will they, under God, refer all. For the writer may assert with respect to both, that the influence of his admonitions will ever be with them to urge them on to all the farther activity and usefulness of which they may be capable. On the departure of his son from England, he accompanied him to Portsmouth, where he gave him his parting blessing—his last *spoken* blessing, for they never met again.

The year 1847 will be long remembered in Great Britain for the misery it entailed, as a year of scarcity, on thousands in all parts of the kingdom. On Wednesday, 24th March, "being the day appointed by her Majesty as a general fast," a solemn service was held, at which he officiated, and pronounced a discourse that was most favorably noticed by both Jewish and Christian press. The sermon was printed by the Mahamad. Another discourse, spoken on the death of Miss Abigail Lindo, authoress of the Hebrew Lexicon, was "so very superior to the usual productions of this kind" that the editor of the *Anglo-Jewish Magazine* published it in his October number, and the editor of *Der Orient*

---

* "Voice of Jacob," vol. iii., No. 74.

deemed it worthy of translating into German.* The only preach-
ers in the London orthodox Synagogues on the occasion above
referred to, we believe, were himself and Dr. Adler, Chief Rabbi
of the German Congregations; and we may state here that with
this respected Rabbi—at whose installation he had assisted—he
always maintained the most friendly relations, as he did with
his predecessor, and with all the leading members of the Ashkenazim.† Thus, it was a source of great satisfaction to him when
Dr. Adler visited the Portuguese Synagogue on Sabbath Besha-
lach, February, 1849, and was entertained at a banquet. On
this occasion, he, in conjunction with the officers of his congregation, gave expression to a most cordial welcome to the respected
guest. But we shall proceed now with our enumeration of a few
of the evidences of his activity, giving them but a brief notice.

In April, 1849, he announced his intention of issuing a second
edition of his translation of the Sephardim Prayers. He added
various new features to this edition, while all the excellencies of
the old were retained. In the first volume, which appeared in
1852, the calendar was continued to the year 1902. The mechanical execution of this edition was, as before, all that could be
desired. It was dedicated to Sir Moses and Lady Montefiore, who
evinced the same interest in this as they did in the first edition. On
the 15th of November of this year, (1849,) "being the day appointed by her Majesty as a general thanksgiving for the removal
of the cholera," he delivered a discourse that was not only published by the Mahamad, but very fully reported in both Jewish
and Gentile journals. His remarks on the exemption of the Jews
from this scourge, and the reasons assigned therefor, based on
references to rabbinical authorities, were particularly noticed;
and suggested a series of articles, written by his son, in the
Canada Medical Journal, on the "Sanitary Institutions of the
Hebrews." In June, 1850, we find him again assisting at the
formation of a Jewish literary society. His address at the pre-

---

* Literatur-Blatt, Jan. 13, 1849.

† Thus, at a meeting when the subject of the admission of certain rejected
deputies was discussed, we find, (*Jewish Chronicle*, 1854), "The Rev. Mr. De
Sola proposed an amendment to leave the matter with the Mahamad to com-
municate with the new Synagogue expressive of the wish of the Sephardim to
be in terms of love and peace with all their brethren."

liminary meeting was specially recommended by the Jewish press
to the consideration of, the friends of the society. His interest
in religious education was farther exhibited in the same month,
when he assisted at the examination of the Jews' Free School;
and about the same time his name was announced by Mr. Mitchell
as one of the adjudicators on the prize essays written for that
gentleman. On Thursday evening, 29th September, 1853, was
consecrated a branch Portuguese Synagogue. The active part
he took in the preparations for this event will be seen by reference to the Jewish press of the day. We may state here, however, that he composed a Hebrew poem for the occasion, that the
melody was also his production, so the translation of the prayers,
and the arrangement of the service. The acknowledgments of
the whole congregation were very cordially conveyed to him.
On Sabbath Yithro of the following year he delivered, at the request of the Mahamad, a sermon "which well deserved to be dif-
fused in wider circles than that to which it was originally addressed." The *Jewish Chronicle* having published it in full, it
was not, like his other published sermons, issued in pamphlet
form by the Mahamad; but they did not fail to convey to him
their acknowledgments, as on former occasions. He contributed
the same year to the Jewish papers, among other pieces, a very
interesting account of the visit of the King of Portugal and suite
to the Portuguese Synagogue at Amsterdam. This communication was read before a meeting of the London Board of Deputies,
who, at the same meeting, took action to bring the claims of the
Jews of Spain before the Cortes. On Thursday, 12th April, 1855,
the Birmingham Hebrew Congregation laid the foundation stone
of their new Synagogue. On this occasion he received from the
executive a special invitation to assist in the arrangement of the
service, the first time that a German Congregation in England
had so honored a Portuguese minister. For this occasion he also
composed a Hebrew ode,* and his services generally, which
afforded the highest satisfaction, were handsomely acknowledged,
and the respects of the congregation duly paid to him at the
banquet succeeding the ceremony. On the completion of the

---

* Reprinted, with a metrical translation in Dutch, in the *Nederlandsch
Israelitische Jaarboekje*, 1857, by Mr. Belinfante.

building,* he revisited Birmingham by invitation to assist at the
consecration, for which he composed another Hebrew ode, and,
as before, met with a most cordial welcome from all. In December
of the same year, he completed a biography of the celebrated
Isaac Samuel Reggio. This was written by him in Dutch, for
the Society "Tot Nut der Israeliten," in the Netherlands, of
which he had been elected an honorary member—an honor then
conferred only on Dr. Sommerhausen, of Brussels, besides himself. This was published in their organ, the *Tijdschrift*, and
covered forty-eight closely printed octavo pages. It was in part
translated into English, for the *Occident* magazine, by Jacob J.
Peres, Professor of Oriental Languages. The same year a former
pupil, Miss Miriam Belisario, issued the prospectus of her "Sabbath Evenings at Home"†—a work of a very high order of merit,
in which she was warmly encouraged and assisted by Mr. De
Sola. She writes she "has submitted her humble efforts to the
religious supervision of the Rev. D. A. De Sola, not feeling herself justified in proffering instruction of such vital importance to
her co-religionists on her own unsanctioned authority." This
work, which was published in two parts, was very well received,
as its utility deserved.

In 1857, Mr. De Sola issued the prospectus of a new work,
entitled "The Ancient Melodies of the Liturgy of the Spanish
and Portuguese Jews," with an Historical Essay on the Poets,
Poetry, and Melodies of this Ritual.‡ For the notation of these
melodies he associated with him Mr. Emanuel Aguilar, an artist
and composer of great eminence, and brother to the lamented
authoress. The prospectus, like all others issued by him, is in
itself of literary value, containing as it does a brief notice of
sacred music in Israel. We cannot now refer to this, but quote
the following to show the design and contents of the publication:

---

* *Tijdschrift van de Maatschappij Tot Nut der Israeliten, deel* iii., No. 4.

† "Sabbath Evenings at Home, or Familiar Conversations on the Jewish
Religion, its Spirit and Observances," by Miriam Mendes Belisario Revised
by the Rev. D. A. De Sola. In two parts. London: S. Joel, 5616–1856.

‡ "The Ancient Melodies of the Liturgy of the Spanish and Portuguese
Jews," harmonized by Emanuel Aguilar, preceded by an Historical Essay,
&c., by the Rev. D. A. De Sola. London: Groombridge & Sons.

At the present day, however, when constant attendance in Synagogue, and the use of Hebrew devotional hymns in private families, once so prevalent among us—and by which means alone these melodies were acquired and orally transmitted—are both much diminished and daily decreasing, it is greatly to be feared that in a few years our sacred music will, for the most part, be entirely forgotten and lost, which, for the reasons mentioned, would indeed be a lamentable and national loss, especially as few among those who have heard these melodies, imperfectly and inharmoniously as they are sung in almost every congregation, can form an adequate idea of their beauty and effect when properly performed, and as we have here endeavored to present them. While these causes still remain, while our choirs are selected from musically untaught persons, while new congregations constantly arise in distant parts of the globe, who, as well as private individuals and families everywhere, would gladly avail themselves of those fine melodies were they known or accessible to them, and are obliged to substitute in their worship new compositions, mostly ill adapted for the sacred purpose they are to subserve, deficient in dignity and solemnity, and incongruous with the rest of the service,—a work, therefore, like the present, which will prevent that loss, possibly remedy that decay, and, in the universal language of music, can address itself and be understood in every clime and country, has assuredly a claim to the support of *all* our co-religionists. For it is not only to our brethren following the Sephardim Ritual that these melodies are solely interesting, or exclusively appertain; even as the sublime hymns to which they are joined, they are the common property of all Israel, and available to them either for public or private devotion. This work will be divided under the following general heads:—1. The most ancient melodies, or those whose origin is supposed to be prior to the settlement of the Jews in Spain. 2. Melodies composed and adapted in Spain, and introduced by them into the various countries in which they took refuge from the persecution of the Inquisition in the Iberian Peninsula. 3. The ancient melodies composed since that period. The most recent of these inserted is at least a century and a half old.

In his learned work, which he styles "An Historical Essay on the Poets, Poetry, and Melodies of the Sephardic Liturgy," and which, as it is the first work of the kind, contains a rich mine for students in this department, introducing them as it does to all the sources, he gives, first, the history of the hymns and poetical pieces inserted in the liturgy of the Sephardim, their structure and peculiarities; secondly, an account of the principal authors of them, and of the times in which they flourished; and, thirdly, he states what he has been able to collect respecting the melodies with which they are combined. He classifies the melodies as follows:—1. Morning hymns, of which he gives six. 2. Sabbath melodies and hymns, of which there are given nineteen; some of these are here translated into English for the first time.

3. Hymns, &c., for New Year and Kippur, of which we have eleven. 4. Festival hymns, of which there are given thirteen. 5. Elegies for Ninth Day of Ab, also thirteen. 6. Occasional hymns, of which there are given eight. There is also an Appendix, containing a new melody for *Adone Olam*, composed by himself, and received with much favor by Sephardic Congregations in England, Holland, and America. The Essay, which is a conversation of most valuable lore, and could only have been written by one who had been a laborious, painstaking student of the subject, drew down upon him most unqualified praise from the Jewish literati of Europe. Jewish and Christian critics alike gave the same verdict. The *Zeitung des Judenthums*, &c., in Germany, the *Tijdschrift*, and also the *Weekblad*, in Holland, re-echo the opinion of the *London Chronicle*, that "the antecedents, the education, and the calling of the author eminently fitted him for the task." The *Athenæum* and the *Literary Gazette* (November 14, 1857), contains elaborate and flattering reviews of the work, as does the *Clerical Journal* (December 8, 1857), and other of the leading scientific and theological magazines. Our limits do not allow us the gratification of showing how these organs of Christian learning and opinion speak of the Jewish minister. In America, Christian critics were not less complementary than the Jewish press; of the latter the Rev. Mr. Leeser's *Occident* contained a review running through three consecutive numbers. The Rev. Mr. Isaacs, of New York, (*Jewish Messenger*,) thanks the author for "his unparalleled essay," which, says the Rev. Dr. Wise, of Cincinnati (*Israelite*), "displays an extraordinary erudition." In London, the well-known William Haslam, in the interesting lecture delivered by him in various parts of England on the "History, Beauties, &c., of the Choral Services of the Synagogue of the Greek, Latin, and Protestant Churches," derives most of the materials of his first lecture "On the Hebrew Service" from this work. In the unique syllabus before us he mentions some ten pieces from Mr. De Sola's work, and adds explanatory notices derived from the same source. One musical piece of Mr. De Sola's composition, the *Adone Olam*, is also selected, and Mr. Haslam styles it "an exquisitely beautiful specimen of modern Jewish music."

On the 26th of December, 1859, he concluded an agreement with Mr. Phillip Vallentine, Hebrew bookseller, who had urged him to undertake for him the translation of the Prayers of the German and Polish Machsor ; and in March of the following year, the first volume of the new edition—the Passover Prayers —appeared.* The space of time thus allowed him was altogether too short for so laborious and difficult a task, especially when his other engagements be taken into consideration; but with this volume, as with the others, the publisher feared a pecuniary loss, unless the work rapidly appeared. The publisher's plan also precluded the addition of notes, rightly deemed by the author indispensable. Some few however were printed at the end of the volumes Mr. De Sola had published, but had never yet been published by another ; he had to acquire a new experience ; and we doubt whether he would ever have consented to write in a similar way again. It is right to state however, that Mr. Vallentine duly performed his part of the agreement, and Mr. De Sola's intercourse with him was always of a perfectly harmonious character, even his protests against the hurry† of his commercial friend being always conveyed in words of jocose remonstrance. We will quote from the Preface to the first volume what he himself says of this work and its difficulties. He reserves, he says, for a future opportunity his observations upon the history and composition of the German and Polish liturgy and continues :—

"When urged to undertake this task, I should not have acquiesced in the proposal, if I had not been promised that my labors should be shared by Mr. M. H. Breslau, a gentleman of well known erudition, from whose able co-operation I undoubtedly expected to derive effective aid. That gentleman, however, soon perceived that the great labor and time which the work would demand to do justice to its importance, would considerably interfere with his other literary engagements, and he consequently felt himself compelled to relinquish his share of the work at its

---

* " The Festival Prayers according to the custom of the German and Polish Jews, with a new English translation, by the Rev. D. A. De Sola. London : P. Vallentine, 5620—1860."

† In a letter, he wittily applies to this undue pressure the text Exod. v. 12— והנגשים אצים לאמר כלו מעשיכם.

very commencement, throwing the whole burden upon myself alone. I must own that I did not form at the outset a correct estimate of the difficulties attendant upon the effort to supply a proper translation of the German *Machsor*. It was only as I proceeded that these difficulties presented themselves successively, until they assumed a character far more formidable than any I had encountered while rendering into the vernacular the prayers of the Sephardic Liturgy. This observation is intended to apply especially to those poetical passages, Piyutim, with which the German Machsor abounds, the difficulties of which will be readily recognised by those who are at all acquainted with the style of the Franco-German school of Hebrew poetry therein found, its ungrammatical and forced construction of the Hebrew—its intermixture of the sacred language with that of the Midrash (the Aramean,) and, though last not least, its brevity and obscurity of expression. These characteristics of the Piyutim rendered a succession of commentaries indispensable, and originated various and very divergent readings according to the peculiar genius of each successive commentator. Hence it is that a vast number of notes are absolutely necessary in order to convey with accuracy the meaning of the poet. But the small size of this edition, and the fact that the Hebrew pages were already cast, precluded me from appending notes for the elucidation of *every* obscure passage; and in many cases I was forced, much to my regret, to consign to the end of the volume indispensable observations, which should have properly accompanied the translation. I very soon found that I could make but little or no use of the version by the late David Levi, unless I wished to propagate his errors both of language and sense, and that consequently it was comparatively easier to make a new translation than to revise and correct his. My labors have however been considerably aided by the perusal and comparison of the able versions found in various continental languages, especially those in German by the celebrated Heidenheim, and the poetical paraphrase of the eloquent and erudite Dr. Michael Sachs. Eminently useful have also proved the Hebrew commentaries on the Piyutim, and the translation of prayers and scriptural passages found in various languages, which were either inaccessible to

David Levi from his non-acquaintance with these languages, or are of a date subsequent to the period in which he lived and labored.   The praise of having been a laborious and conscientious translator cannot be denied to that learned individual; but it must be equally admitted by all that his version is often inelegant and obscure.   *   *   *   As after these remarks the reader will naturally be surprised at seeing portions of Levi's translation in these pages, I deem it necessary to declare here, what will be found reiterated throughout the work, that I positively declined to translate what Heidenheim, and others had omitted from their versions; but the proprietor preferred to employ Levi's rendering of those passages to the alternative of leaving them untranslated as in the continental editions.   Every such passage will be found emphatically designated."

The reviews of this work were of a very flattering character, but we shall merely quote the opinion of the ripe Hebrew scholar, since deceased, to whom Mr. De Sola refers in the Preface as his intended *collaborateur*.   Mr. Breslau in his "Hebrew Review" vol. i, p. 754, says " The translation is replete with remarkable improvements upon every previous version in the English language, manifesting good judgment and excellent taste.   Having ourselves labored in this field of literature, we can appreciate the difficulties of the task to render cabalistic, astrological and allegorical ideas in which the Piyutim abound, so as to be intelligible to a modern reader, and to make sound sense of the composition in which propriety and devotional sentiment have been sacrificed to rhyme.   This task has been most ably and skilfully performed by the Rev. D. A. De Sola, coping with the difficulty of producing a nearly faithful yet judicious version, and for which the reverend translator is entitled to the unqualified gratitude of the advocates of the Piyutim *in toto*."

Besides the works already mentioned, he produced others of lesser magnitude.   We will presently give a list of these; but first we would proceed to show that they were not the productions of a man of leisure, but of one whose every hour was demanded by numerous other engagements and actual official duties.

The indisposition of the Sephardim in England to establish any other but their venerable Synagogue in Bevis Marks formed the community, until recently, into but one large congregation, greatly increased by an almost daily accession of adherents to the Minhag from all parts of the world—the number of this floating population being in fact considerably larger than that of the residents. The births, deaths and marriages in such a congregation would necessarily occupy a considerable portion of his time, dispersed as his constituents were miles distant from the synagogue and his residence.* And besides attendance twice—in the early summer three times a day in the Synagogue—he was also *Hazan of Hebra*,† and as such required by the Ascama "to accompany to the grave every deceased person, and say prayers at the house of mourners who may require it morning and evening during the seven days of *Abel*." In the winter months he was required to attend at least twice a week at the *Medras* for the study of *Harambam*, &c. Here the good sense and proper temper which characterized his share of the discussions were pre-eminent. Instruction in the Hebrew language, literature and religion also occupied no inconsiderable portion of his time. Indeed, his residence may have been regarded as a kind of normal school whereat many a Jewish minister, some now in office both in England and the colonies—the writer gratefully includes himself among them—obtained their chief training.‡ Besides his private engagements which were very numerous, his services were in acquisition at various times in the leading schools of Solomons, Neumegen, Cohen, &c., and for many years were regularly continued at the well-known and excellent establishment of the Belisarios at Clapton. The in-

---

* A communication made jointly with his colleague, Hazan Almosnino to the Velhos, says: "It is notorious that the numerous duties of the Hazanim require the devotion of the whole of their time, since they are always liable to be called upon for the performance of some of their duties," &c.

† It was probably in virtue of this office that we find him assisting at a Presentation by that pious confraternity the "Lavadores," to their venerable brother Sir Moses Montefiore, (Jew. Chron. xii. 15,)—the meetings of the brethren being generally of an exclusive character. The Manual of the Brethren presented by Hermano Isaac Jalfon, Esq., adopts his translation of the Psalms.

‡ His youngest son Samuel, the present talented and very promising Junior Incumbent of K. K. Shaar Ashamaim is no exception to this statement.

terest he took in the communal schools was evinced by his frequent presence on private as well as public occasions—on the latter he was generally requested to act as Examiner. In the schools of his own congregation, his interest was of a more anxious and special character. This is evidenced in the representations made by him from time to time to the Elders and others.* The secular education of the community also greatly engaged his attention. Fully appreciating the exclusiveness of Oxford and Cambridge, he was among the earliest advocates of the non-sectarian London University, and when the corporation proposed the establishment of "The City of London School" on a comprehensive and liberal basis in 1834, besides sending his own sons among the earliest pupils, he gave it his most zealous co-operation. But the corporeal as well as the spiritual and mental wants of his flock required his time and attention. His office of Hazan of Hebra brought him necessarily in contact with much misery and want. To make himself acquainted with such cases, and to relieve them through their more fortunate brethren, he always used his best endeavors. Besides the lamented Lady Judith Montefiore, there were other noble daughters of Israel, some still living, who would not desire their names to be divulged, who determined upon a systematic scheme of relief, by issuing privately through Mr. De Sola tickets for food, clothing and fuel. The issue of tickets was specially made on Fridays, when his residence presented rather the appearance of a public office than a private dwelling. "The Sephardim Ladies' Relief Society," on the Committee of which were his daughters,† received its full share of his sympathy and aid. He was one of the first projectors of that excellent Institution "The Soup Kitchen for Jewish Poor," and the interest he took in this his favorite charity was indeed very great. He was a permanent member of the Committee, was seldom absent from its distributions, and always contributed as liberally as he could to its funds. His literary labors took him much to the Library of

* See his Plan, &c., for Jewish Normal School and letter to the Velhos; also his address on the laying of the foundation Stone of the National Infant School, 5603.

† Heb. Observer, Dec. 9, 1853.

the British Museum, and he was also a daily visitor at the London Institution, where besides the library, there were the best issues of the Periodical Press to claim his attention. Literary men whether of great or lesser reputation, and from all quarters had their drafts to present on his leisure; but there was nothing in which he so much delighted as this intellectual converse, and he sacrificed much to it. There were few Jewish literati in England or on the Continent, who did not become acquainted with him—and by all was he respected and esteemed. The same may be said of his intercourse with Christians, which was very extensive.* We are in possession of quite a mass of correspondence chiefly from the most eminent Jewish scholars, all of a purely literary character, and so valuable as well to deserve publication, more especially the communications of Drs. Jost, Delitsch, Fürst, Zunz, Rapoport, Asher, &c., in Germany; Beliufante, Isaacson, Bassan, &c., in Holland; Carmoly, Cohen, &c., in France; Loewe, Zedner, Raphall, Dukes, Picciotto, and numerous others in England.† We notice particularly the correspondence of Dr. Jost, because it refers to a design that learned man had to publish an English translation of the History of the Jews, under the editorial care of Mr. De Sola. The so-called "Prospectus" of the proposed publication contains six closely written folio pages. The learned Doctor imparted his design while on a visit chiefly undertaken for the purpose to Mr. De Sola in 1841. We are not quite certain of the reason why this important undertaking was abandoned. It need scarcely be said that this elaborate prospectus is of great literary interest. With reference to

---

* We cannot deprive ourself of the pleasure of especially mentioning Colonel Moody of Waltham Abbey, Rev. George Beckel, Captain Boyse, Messrs. W. G. Dresser, and the Brothers Frost.

† Many communications are in Hebrew, with copies of his replies. One, *exempli gratia*, written by him to Dr. Isaacson, Chief Rabbi of the German Community in Rotterdam, on the subject of גרים displays a facile Hebrew pen and great Talmudic learning. One letter is written (mirabile dictu!) in good Hebrew, by a young lady co-religionist, the late worthy Abigail Lindo, when sending him a presentation copy of her Hebrew Dictionary. Here we may add that the large number of presentation copies sent to him from all quarters, but more especially from Germany, shows the high esteem in which he was held.

it Dr. Jost writes (Frankfort, o. M., September 7, 1841): "If it does not entirely displease you, there is permission given to you both to change phrases and expressions as you like best, or to add whatever you may think to the purpose." Next we might refer to the communications of Mr. A. Asher. This gentleman, his warm admirer and friend, the accomplished translator and annotator of Benjamin of Tudela, was head of the well-known firm of Asher & Co., one of the most extensive publishing houses in Berlin. Mr. Asher was accustomed to make periodic visits—always a source of extreme pleasure to Mr. De Sola and his family,—chiefly to make collections of rare Hebrew and Oriental works for the Prussian government. On these occasions he gladly availed himself of the great bibliographical knowledge of Mr. De Sola, and was the means of making him known to Bunsen and other German celebrities. Some of the most important acquisitions of Mr. Asher,* who also collected for the British Museum, were in consequence of his friend's aid and advice. The gratitude of Mr. Asher was shown by sending him everything that appeared in Germany in the domain of Jewish literature. In this connection it may be stated, that bibliographers were accustomed to send, to Mr. De Sola scarce and valuable works for his notice and opinion, and he collected for his own library many rare printed books and MSS., some of great literary value.†

A further examination of such of his correspondence as is still preserved shows the lively interest he took in all the important Jewish questions of the day, and this without limit of language or country. Thus we find Chief Rabbi Adler thanking him "for his lucid and ample description in his valuable letter which Dr. Adler would forward to the Chief Rabbi of Gaya." Various letters from Sir Moses Montefiore, acknowledge in cordial terms

---

* Among them was that valuable MS. the מחזור בקלף איהלקי in two folio volumes.

† They contain the Spanish (fol.) *Verdad de la ley de Moseh*, a curious collection of Spanish, Portuguese MSS., a beautifully written copy of the Portuguese Prayers in English, &c. One very valuable Spanish MS., of a controversial character, he obtained for the late Gershom Kursheedt. (See *Occident*, vol. xvii, No. 23.

various translations and other literary labors performed by him, and expressing at the same time sentiments of peculiar regard. We find Baron Rothschild thanking him on one occasion "for his communication which would aid the good cause in the prosecution of his just rights and in the vindication of civil and religious liberty," and again addressing him upon "certain misrepresentations in the House of Commons so clearly and fully refuted by the information from Holland which Mr. De Sola has taken the trouble to obtain." Another subject which seems to have been very dear to him was the return of his co-religionists to Spain and Portugal. Here we find some most interesting information imparted by his friend Joshua Benoliel. From the United States* we have a large number of communications on a variety of topics, some as far back as the first Reform movement in Charleston. Glancing through others, we find here a commission from the Antipodes to select the materials for a Jewish library in Sydney, there a commission from Canada to present a congratulatory address from the Jews of Montreal to the first Jewish Lord Mayor of London. From the West Indies, instruction and advice are sought on certain doctrinal points.†

---

* The late Solomon Solis, the able contributor to the *Occident*, was a frequent visitor at Mr. De Sola's during his stay in England. The writer well remembers how earnestly he sought opinion and information from Mr. De Sola on a topic he was then discussing in the *Occident*—the Immortality of the Soul.

† There is a characteristic letter from the well known B. C. Carillon. After thanking him " with heartfelt gratitude" for aiding him to discharge a filial duty, he refers to Mr. De Sola's Bible translation as a gigantic undertaking, and continues " to translate well that interesting portion of Scripture (the Prophets) demands thorough theologians. To render it as it should be, a perfect knowledge of the Hebrew grammar is but the least requirement. A scholar is not yet a theologian, and if I grant that besides yourself, Mr. Raphall and a few others, there be many perfect Hebrew scholars in England, yet will that enable them to translate the Prophets? To do so they ought not only to be *well-trained theologians*, but also *Poets*, and they must have entered into the spirit of the sacred Poetry. Moreover a mere translation, without proper illustrations, is as good as nothing. Your plan is the best made within the last fifty years, and I therefore beseech you to proceed with it. Were I to translate the Bible I would follow the example of the old Targumim and that of Mendelssohn, by giving at once the true meaning of the original in the translation; for unless we paraphrase we give

From Belgium he receives from the Jewish Literary Society a highly complimentary letter, accompanying his Diploma as Honorary member. From his native Holland the communications are quite voluminous, chiefly from the learned J. J. Belinfante, to whose magazines he was an industrious contributor.* Next we perceive various Hebrew letters, chiefly calls for material aid and sympathy from distant Asia and Africa, and nearer home we find not a few letters of thanks from Jewish authors for literary assistance rendered, or for aid in circulating their works. Among these we find the names of almost every Anglo-Jewish writer, besides a large number from abroad. The editors of the Jewish Journals also acknowledge their indebtedness to him for occasional assistance and translations from the various foreign Jewish periodicals, such as the Hebrew " Hamagid," the Spanish " Shaarai Misrach," the Italian " Cronica Israelita," the French " Archives Israelites," the Dutch " Tijdschrift," the German " Orient," Zeitung des Judenthums, &c. Indeed his extensive attainments as a linguist were brought into request not only in this manner, but some of the principal Proctors of Doctors Commons, Mr. De Pinna and other votaries, were for many years accustomed to avail themselves of his services for important translations. The number and variety of subjects whereon he is addressed by Christian writers is truly curious; clergy and laity alike propound questions in Philology, Biblical Archæology, Jewish Antiquities, History, &c.—frequently with a view of evolving Jewish opinion on the great moral movements of the day, such as the Temperance Question, and his replies have been embodied in their works.† The writer himself records

but the dead letter without the spirit. I have myself already rendered in that manner several chapters of Isaiah and would undertake to finish it; but what can we do in the West Indies? Were I in England, I would assist you in convincing our English brethren, that if they be richer, because they live among the greatest commercial nation of the present time, yet can they not cope with the Dutch and German Jews in knowledge, and least of all in theological knowledge."

* His co-religionists in his native city always evinced great interest and pride in him. Mr. J. J. Belinfante in his "Sketch of Jewish writers since Mendelssohn," which appeared in the quarterly Tijdschrift, No. 3, Amsterdam, 1851, refers to him in a most complimentary manner and gives a long account of his activity. See also Leerrede door A. C. Carillon, Amsterdam, 1833, and an article on " The Anglo-Jewish Writers," in the Nederlandsch Israelitische Jaarboekje, 1855.

† See among others " The Strong Drink Question," " Total Abstinence harmonized with Scripture." &c.

as a duty his undying gratitude for the instruction and aid he has obtained from him in the solution of doubts on many theological and scientific points. His communications received from 1847 to 1860, and which have been preserved, would be regarded by every Hebrew student as exceedingly valuable and interesting. They created one of those debts for which there can be no return. From various MS. Addresses, Funeral Discourses, Reports of Committees drafted by him, and printed notices, we perceive that of late years much of his time must have been devoted to the service of the Masonic fraternity, of which he was a highly esteemed member and the respected chaplain of the Joppa Lodge. The published report of a celebration of the exalted Joppa Royal Arch Chapter styles him "Companion" of the Chapter.* It might be supposed that so many engagements would necessarily narrow his leisure in the family and social circles. But this was not so. He was eminently of a social disposition and gathered around him not merely a number of acquaintances, but of warm friends, who deemed it a privilege to draw nearer yet in their intercourse with one so highly gifted and, yet withal, so remarkably unassuming. The writer will not essay to describe him fully in the family circle. Venerated and idolized by his children, time has only served to develop the wide and desolate extent of their loss. There is not a shadow, however faint, to darken the bright, even if tearful, memories of this best of parents. Specially dignified in manner as in personal appearance, he was yet most indulgent to all short-comings, most patient in his teachings, and was wont to reprove not with severity, but by some wise and witty saying, or some humorous etching of his ever ready pencil. To promote the happiness and welfare of his children was the great study and main effort of his life. Around the cheerful fireside he would gather with them and the dear partner of his cares, and, putting aside the graver engagements and studies of the day, would become a very child among children, interested in all their occupations, participating in all their amusements, turning, it might be, from the profound pages of a Maimonides and Abarbanel to read aloud to them the sayings of Sam Weller and Mr. Pickwick. But here is a topic

---

* Jew. Chron. vi. 37, xiv. 137, &c.

we may not continue. Days made happy by his ever considerate love and improved by his ever watchful care, peaceful Sabbaths, joyous festivals and merry anniversaries, alike speak out from the tomb of the past with their tender memories on which the mind loves to dwell not unpleasurably.

We now append the list of his works to which we before referred :

IN HEBREW.

I. סדר התפלות כמנהג כפרדים חלק א'

II. אגרות לחכמי זכננו כ"י

III. * אלה בני הנעורים של לוצאטו הוגה בשקידה רבה כ"י

IV. שיר תודה ביום חנוך בהכ' החרשה לק"ק כפרדים בלונדן

V. קול רנה ביום הונח לארץ אבן פנת בהכ' החרשה לק"ק בירמינגהם

VI. שיר תודה ביום חנוך בהכ' הנ"ל

---

* We extract from one of his ordinary communications to us the following, respecting this delightful production, of Luzzato, which he has enriched with learned critical notices. * * " A work unique in its kind. The original edition was printed by him (Luzzato) in London ; but as only one hundred copies were struck off, it has quite disappeared. Even the British Museum and Oxford Libraries do not possess a copy. It was however reprinted by Satnov some years ago but full of errors, and with omissions of a great many of the Poems. Having had it lent to me by Dr. Van Ovan (in 1824), I copied it. Its literary merit I need not enlarge upon. It is the best work of its kind, and is sufficiently known and celebrated as such. I have written an article on E. Luzzato in " Der Orient." You will find it entitled "De Sola über Ephraim Luzzato." The following is his record of the time (פרט) when he finished this work :—

ותהי השלכת העתקת הספר הזה בסימן טוב וכבורך ביום רביעי כ' לחרש חשון
שנת שכרה עלי לפ"ק

To the original title he adds the following :—

נדפס בלונדון יע"א על ירי G. Richardson & S. Clark בשנת 1766 לחשבונם
והעתקתי אותו ליוקר חשיבותו ונם כי אינו בנמצא אני הצעיר דוד בכ"ר אהרן די
כולה : כ"ן דור יהיה כעזרי וביער כל אשר לי אכן :

IN HEBREW AND ENGLISH.

VII. סדר ברכות "The Blessings," with Introductory Essay on Thanksgiving, 1 vol., 1829.

VIII. כדר התפלות "Forms of Prayer," of the Portuguese Minhag, new Translation with Notes and Calendar for Fifty Years, &c., 6 vols., 1836.

IX. Second edition of the same, with additions, &c., 6 vols., 1852.

X. כפר בראשית "The Sacred Scriptures," new Translation with copious Notes, in conjunction with Dr. Raphall, Genesis, 1 vol., 1844.

XI. מחזור למועדי ה' "Festival Prayers," according to the German and Polish Minhag, 4 vols., 1860.

IN ENGLISH.

XII. "The Mishna," conjointly with Dr. Raphall. A portion (Eighteen Treatises) of this work was published by Mr. B. Elkin, 1 vol., 1845.

XIII. The Sacred Scriptures, English edition, 1 vol., 1843.

XIV. The Ancient Melodies of the Liturgy of the Spanish and Portuguese Jews, 1 vol., 1857.

XV. The Cheap Jewish Library, edited and revised for Charlotte Montefiore, 2 vols., 1841.

XVI. Sabbath Evenings at Home, edited and revised for Miriam Belisario, 2 parts, 1856.

XVII. Sermons delivered on various occasions in K. K. Shaar Ashamaim, London, 8 vols., MS.

XVIII. Sermons printed by the Mahamad, &c.

XIX. Three Lectures delivered before the Jewish Literary Society—"Moses the Prophet, Moses Maimonides and Moses Mendelssohn, MS.

XX. Contributions to the Oriental Review, 1836-40.

XXI. Contributions to the Hebrew Review of Dr. Raphall.

XXII. Sermons on the Decalogue, from the German of Dr. Salomon, (incomplete) MS.

XXIII. "The Proper Names in the Scriptures," 1837.

XXIV. Detailed Calendar, being Tables for Fifty Years, &c., 5594-5644, MS.

XXV. "A Common Place Book," in which a variety of subjects are contained, extracts from rare books, &c., MS.

XXVI. Address to the Israelites of Great Britain, MS.

XXVII. On the Establishment of a Jewish Normal School, Plan and explanatory remarks, MS.

XXVIII. Notes on Basnago and Milman's History of the Jews, MS.

XXIX. Contributions to the Anglo-Jewish periodicals.

XXX. Miscellanies, some minor pieces in MS. e. g. on the discussion of Sam. xix. 13, in the Hebrew Review; Translation of the Preface of the Chizuk Emunah, for a translation of that work made by the writer, on the Legend of the Wandering Jew. A Scheme of Alterations of the Pregaos in Synagogue, and for some necessary authorized alterations in the mode of performing divine service; the Jewish Commentators on the Nazir and Temperance Question. On the Exile of the Jews of Spain. A translation of Aben Ezra's Poem on Chess, made for Alexandre, &c., &c.

IN GERMAN.

XXXI. Contributions to the Algemeine Zeitung des Judenthums, 1836–1845.

XXXII. Biography of Distinguished Israelites in England.

XXXIII. Biography of Ephraim Luzzato.

XXXIV. Contributions to the Orient.

IN DUTCH.

XXXV. Biography of Reggio (pamphlet).

XXXVI. Correspondence with J. J. Belinfante, MS.

XXXVII. Historical Account of Jewish Periodicals from the latter half of the last century till the present day.

XXXVIII. Biography of Grace Aguilar.

XXXIX. Contributions to the Quarterly Magazine of the "Society for the Benefit of the Israelites in the Netherlands, published at the Hague.

XL. Contributions to the Ned. Isr. Jaarbock.

With the above list, we close our very incomplete notice of his literary activity, and having essayed to give a sketch equally imperfect, of the manner in which he discharged the various duties and relations of life, it remains for us now but to speak of the final close of a career not less honorable to the house of Israel than to himself. In the middle of August, 1860, he was attacked with erysipelas in his left hand and arm, and after a week of intense suffering received permission from his physician to go to Ramsgate for the benefit of the sea air. In a communication written to us at this time, he refers to the pressure put upon him to hurry the completion of the translation of the German Prayers on which he was then engaged, though able to use one hand only. He was translating the concluding service of Kipur—a strangely appropriate subject for the conclusion of his labors—and writes: "I have had to do this enormous and difficult work single-handed, without the slightest assistance, and I cannot turn out anything to which my name is attached unless it be as well done as it is in my power to make it. I fear, though, that I have worked too much at it. * * * I am now at the נעילה and must work unceasingly at it, even with one hand, until it is finished."* The work *was* finished before the holydays, just as the publisher had sought of him. He had worked on in pain, or in intervals of relief, until he arrived at the last words uttered on the holy Kipur day—words which are also the last syllabled with the failing breath of the dying Israelite. With these most solemn words he closed his literary labors, never more to resume them.

He returned from the sea-shore to be in town during the holydays; but a month's suffering had so reduced him that he was unable to officiate even on the sacred day of Kipur—and this being for the first time in forty-three years, caused him the deepest grief. With the arrival of the Succot feast, he felt sufficiently recovered to officiate, but was deterred from doing so, by the kind remonstrances of his friends. He spent the holyday evening in the family tabernacle, as he had been accustomed for

---

* He saw no revise of the four volumes translated by him, which were unfortunately shorn of his valuable explanatory notes by the too contracted plan of the publisher.

nearly half a century; but this, it was thought, was most unfortunate, as probably too long a stay there assisted to develope, or perhaps laid the germs of the disease which subsequently proved fatal. Symptoms appeared which were pronounced by his physicians to be rheumatic fever, and he was again advised to leave town. He, however, assisted in the morning service of Simhat Torah, one of his sons-in-law being the Hatan of the day. With this is connected a circumstance of remarkable character. When the law had been taken out, to the surprise of many and delight of all, he advanced to the Teba, and after a silence of so many weeks, his voice was once more heard within those holy walls commencing *" This is the blessing wherewith Moses the man of God blessed the children of Israel before his death."* The manner in which he chanted this last portion of the law, we are assured, will never be forgotten by those who heard him. No sick man's voice was that which now, with so much energy and so much sweetness, thrilled through every nerve of his hearers. The whole congregation were electrified with a delivery of which their Hazan had not been capable in the best days of his youth and strength. Yet many besides his relatives shed tears, for it prognosticated to them that they were hearing him for the last time; and it was of general remark after the service had concluded, that it appeared as if he was addressing that blessing to his congregation as his own final benediction to them. When leaving the Synagogue, all crowded around him to offer their congratulations at seeing him again at his post; and at the banquet in the Vestry chamber which succeeded, all the speakers expressed the delight they felt in having once more heard his revered voice. These evidences of the warm love of his flock greatly affected him. He had seemed overjoyed to be again at the Teba; but with the departure of the holydays all joys and cares were for him to fade away. And here let it be permitted us to say, that, if we are dwelling somewhat fully in describing his last hours, we do so because they were so edifying, so indicative of true piety and resignation, that we deem it not less right than profitable to recall them. His disease daily continued to make cruel progress, the most eminent physicians in London were summoned, who pronounced his condition to be

most perilous, and they directed his removal to Shacklewell.
On the Thursday—four days before he was freed—it was announced to his family that his case was hopeless. On the same
day he calmly inquired of one of his physicians if he thought
him *in extremis*, and with equal calmness received the announce-
ment that he ought immediately to arrange his earthly affairs.
But always understanding the frail tenure of human life, he had
long since set his house in order, as pious Jews will. His only
remark, some time after was " What am I better than my ancestors?"—either applying these words to the shortness of his life,
(he was then in his sixty-fourth year) or following out some other
train of thought. He called his family to him, and in all their grief
—controlled before him—it was matter of wonder to them how
clear and collected he was speaking to them and acquainting
them with his last wishes. He desired his son-in-law, Rev. Mr.
Mendes, who was present, to read the *Vidui*, the last solemn
confessions, with him ; and when the reader faltered, he urged
him on by repeating from memory every word. His last Sabbath on earth approached. He had greatly suffered on the
Friday, but towards dusk he remarked to his children around
him that it was Friday evening, and inquired whether their
mother had lit the Sabbath light. He was asked if he would
like to make the Kidush; and the bread being cut for him, he
said the Sanctification word for word in his old manner—though
those around him had the agony of knowing that they were
listening to the well-known words for the last time—that the
most hallowed associations of many years were to be rent asun-
der, and that they should no more bend their heads to receive
his blessing as they were used on those peaceful and happy
Friday nights. He maintained his consciousness throughout
the Sabbath, though he suffered acutely ; and desirous that
his children should not be harrowed by witnessing his suf-
ferings, called them singly to him and dismissed them with
his blessing. Not less fervently did he bestow his last blessing
on his absent children in America, and on his eldest daughter
who was prevented by sickness from being there. On the Sun-
day he was still conscious and repeated from memory several
Psalms and the *Vidui*, with his attached friend Mr. Benoliel,

who, like many others, sought as highest privilege to join in the last prayers of such a man. Indeed, so soon as it became known there was no more hope, the utmost consternation and deepest grief seized his congregation and friends who found it impossible to realize that he was going from them. The house of Shacklewell was crowded by anxious inquirers and those desiring to see him yet once more, and to aid and comfort his family.

His colleague, the Rev. Mr. Piza, who always looked up to him with the esteem and reverence of a son, could not be persuaded to leave his bedside, day or night. So with the venerable Solomon Almosnino, and other equally devoted friends of both sexes. "Feeling," writes one, to express the sentiments of all, "that I was losing a dear friend and adviser, whom I loved as if nature had bound me to him, I remained near him to the end." The nearer that end approached the more anxious did he become to be removed to his old home, which adjoined the Synagogue. This was his constant request, but it was one which his family saw in their grief might not be granted him. His mind seemed to settle almost entirely on the one point, that the final separation of soul and body might be in closest possible proximity to the old Synagogue—near the hallowed spot where the greater part of his life had been piously spent. This was his almost sole articulation, unless when he joined in the prayers so solemnly offered by the Ministers near him; and when the last *Shemang* was pronounced, it was a beautiful and edifying sight to witness how his face lighted up as he repeated it after them. The last word he uttered was the Almighty's name; and he was not, for God took him.

He was freed on Monday, the thirteenth day of Heshvan, (29th October) 5621, at about five minutes before eight o'clock. At the same hour there was commenced in the Shaär Ashamain Synagogue the ordinary morning service, the first words of which are, "*My God, the soul which thou hast given me is pure; thou takest it from me, but restorest it to me in futurity.*" The young reader knew not that the pure soul of his revered Minister, a few miles distant, had just departed, to commence in a state of greater purity yet, and among the higher intelligences, its adorations of the ADON KOL HANESHAMOT.

If any thing could alleviate the grief of his distracted family it was the extraordinary respect shown to his memory on all sides, and that their sorrow was shared by so many. The authorities of the congregation did all they possibly could to evince their affectionate esteem for their late Minister. They determined that every thing consistent with the last wishes of the deceased—for he had prohibited all funeral pomp in his will—should be done to invest with befiting dignity the last tribute they could offer to one who had so long and devotedly ministered to their highest interests. They proceeded to Shacklewell, where the brethren of the Lavadores took charge of his honored remains and removed him to his old home. The melancholy cortege at its return was met with general evidences of regret and grief. On the day of the funeral, an immense assembly, swelled with the arrival of friends from long distances, filled the neighborhood, Jew and Gentile alike desirous of exhibiting a last token of respect to one they deemed so worthy of it. And in that mixed crowd of rich and poor, learned and untaught, orthodox and reformers, the prevalent exclamation was, not how great a scholar, but how good a man, had left them. Some threescore mourning and private carriages followed the hearse, some sent by the Masonic body* who with the various societies and the general public formed an immense procession, such as few there had ever witnessed. Those most solemn obsequies which the Sephardim are accustomed to accord to their departed Hazanim were proceeded with, participated in by Ministers of all Synagogues; and amidst the solemn chants which left no heart untouched and no eye tearless, the honored dead was carried from the scene of his past labors; from the place and people he had so greatly loved in life. Unable to control their emotion, strong men stepped aside to weep like children. And when the sad rites were completed, all turned from his grave with the indelible consciousness that there had been deposited a man of extraordinary moral worth, of unsullied principles, distinguished for all those amiable qualities that grace humanity; one who had ever done honor to the office he held, as

---

* A solemn Masonic funeral service was subsequently (on the 4th November) performed in honor of his memory. Brother Berkowitz officiating on the mournful occasion.

he had been the pride and ornament of the congregation he had so long and faithfully served. Thoroughly assured that he had gone to reap the reward of his many virtues, as son, husband, parent and Israelite, deeply touched hearts dictated to willing lips the words of the inspired page, "Let me die the death of the righteous, and let my last end be like his!"

We do not refer to the eulogiums which the press, the resolutions of various societies and letters of condolence from all quarters alike bestowed on his memory,* but we close our willingly imposed task by subjoining some remarks with which we have been favored by one who was neither related to him nor a member of his flock, but who was a dispassionate observer of his course. Mr. J. L. Levison, the erudite author of "Mental Culture,"† thus writes of him.

*   *   *   "The deceased had indeed much of the *suaviter in modo*, and yet he was not deficient in the *fortiter in re;* for he acted with a steadiness of purpose on all occasions."

"Although a good linguist and biblical student with many official duties to perform and the care and anxiety consequent on a large family, yet he always appeared cheerful. And we especially noticed that he manifested much quiet good-tempered wit, without any tinge of ill humor; and although he could excite the risible muscles of his associates on such occasions, that he did so without leaving any unpleasant recollections to rankle in the memory; for he was never malicious or personal. His ample and active natural benevolence interposed to prevent either harshness or malevolence; consistently religious himself, he did not act with

---

*Not the least prized by his family were the feeling eulogistic addresses delivered in the vestry chamber, the kind consideration manifested toward his widow and children, and the immediate appointment of his youngest son to an almost similar office.

† We quote from Mr. Levison's kind communication.

"In a recent conversation with your brother, he incidentally mentioned that you were preparing an account of the life and literary labors of your late esteemed father, (peace to his soul, Amen,) and he said that you would not object to insert a few memoranda, which I had jotted down after attending his funeral."

Westridge Villa, St. John's Wood.

asperity or vindictiveness to those who were lax, but he would give some apposite anecdote, the moral of which might convey a covert reproof or not, as he left it to the sagacity of his hearers to form their own inference.

"We have visited him at his own house, where surrounded by his amiable partner and family he appeared the same considerate being, and when he addressed young or old, all were impressed with a feeling of esteem from his good-heartedness and consideration.

"Modest, as all true scholars are said to be, he spoke not as if he were a master, but as a student interchanging ideas with a kindred companion. Such a state of mind is a surety that he had cultivated his moral attributes with his intellectual powers. Possessing a tendency to study individualities of minds, we had noticed the peculiar traits of the Rev. D. A. De Sola, and had marked the influence of certain combinations of his mental powers in the formation of his own individuality of character. Thus we are assured that he possessed both strong feelings and moral sentiments, and these conjointly gave to his religious professions their practical tendency. As husband, father, and friend, he was both considerate and kind. His humor partook more of the playfulness of a happy, child-like spirit, trying to throw off worldly cares from his own mind and from the minds of those with whom he associated.

"Other observations presented him to us under graver aspects, and yet under even such circumstances he invariably preserved his cordial and unostentatious character, and was, therefore, always the true gentleman. We also often noticed, that though himself a scholar and thinker, yet he could make himself perfectly intelligible to those who had no pretensions to learning, and that, when he addressed such persons, he did not offend their egotism, but used the most unpedantic terms and assumed a quiet, colloquial manner. It was the latter traits that invariably brought to our minds the words which Moses Mendelssohn addressed to the surviving brother of Lessing,—we quote from memory,— 'Your brother had the capacity to impart knowledge in such a simple and natural manner, that those who were the recipients of his information could scarcely distinguish the fact whether they had or had not themselves excogitated the new ideas, and thus he was unlike some of the rich who, when they confer favors, make us feel the weight of the obligations we incur,—he, on the contrary, bestowed his mental wealth so generously that, in appropriating it, we became unconscious of the source from which we had received it.'

"This faculty of giving generously his thoughts for the benefit of others, we had often observed in our late esteemed friend, even in a promiscuous conversation. And that he would make the most erudite remarks or give some curious antiquarian information without any one having his feelings compromised from the absence of any thing like egotism on his part.

"It must not be supposed that he was not greatly appreciated. At the last sad scene of suffering humanity, where 'the body is returned to the earth and the spirit to the God who gave it,' there were unmistakable proofs how much he was beloved and respected, as the aspect of that large assembly had a sadness of expression as if some one near akin had departed from each of them.

"We have not entered into any details confirmatory of the above mentioned statements, as, in all probability, the learned Editor will supply many illustrative facts to confirm their accuracy. This he will do from a deep sense of filial love and to do justice to one who had devoted his life to elucidate and instruct his contemporaries in their duties, which as Israelites they owe to God, to their faith, and as members of the community. And we believe that he indeed practised what he taught."